I refuse to be scared.

His leap in my direction is even faster than I expect. Only the fact that I am uphill keeps him from reaching me, and the loose stones that he slips on are all that stop him from catching up to me. I turn and scramble back up the slope as fast as I can, the bearwalker close behind me, my death in his enraged eyes.

BEARWALKER

BEARWALKER

JOSEPH BRUCHAC

Illustrations by
Sally Wern Comport

SCHOLASTIC INC.
New York Toronto London Auckland
Sydney Mexico City New Delhi Hong Kong

ISBN 978-0-545-32195-2

16 15 14   20 21/0

Printed in the U.S.A.   40

First Scholastic printing, November 2010

To my sons, Jim and Jesse—
who have followed the tracks
of many bears

CONTENTS

Prologue

'm writing this in my journal as I lean against an old hemlock. I'm not bleeding so much now and the writing helps me focus my mind and not fall asleep. I can't allow myself to fall asleep. I have to keep my eyes and ears open. Otherwise he might creep up on me.

People talk a lot about good and evil. Some say that no one is born bad. It's just a result of the way they were raised. But that's not what my ancestors believed. Some beings, some animals and people—and those who are both human and animal at the same time—are *otgont*, twisted away from the path of the good mind. All they care for is power and they're always hungry. The way he is.

Did I hear a twig crack? I listen, but I don't hear anything. And that is not such a good sign. On a night like this, when the moon is bright enough for me to see the pages of my notebook and write in it, there are usually sounds in the woods. Unless something big is out there hunting. Then everything gets this quiet—as quiet as I am trying to be. Quiet enough that the Bearwalker won't find me.

My uncle Jules told me about the Bearwalker. Long ago, he said, there was a Mohawk village. One day people began to disappear. They would go out hunting or to work in the fields and never return. Were enemies ambushing them? Was it some big animal that attacked silently and then carried off their bodies? No one knew.

Then one day a hunter found something that filled him with fear. He ran back to the village to tell everyone.

"I saw the tracks of a huge bear," he said.

"We have all seen bear tracks before," another hunter said. "What is so special about bear tracks?"

"Ah," the first man said, a shiver of fear going down his back as he spoke, "these were no ordinary tracks. For as I followed them they became the tracks of a man."

A long silence descended then upon the people. They all understood now why people had been vanishing. They knew now what creature had come to prey upon their people. It was the one they called a monster bear, one of those *otgont* beings, neither human nor animal, but a terrible mixture of both. It could take the form of a human or the shape of a great bear. But unlike a *real* human or bear, it lived only for blood and death. Perhaps this creature had once been a human, but his lust for power had been so great that he had done the things needed to transform him into a monster bear. One of those things (and this sent a chill down my back when Uncle Jules whispered the words) was to sacrifice the life of one of his own relatives.

When it seemed human, the monster bear spoke with a voice that was pleasing, so pleasing that it would confuse those who heard it and they would follow this tall, attractive human without thinking, follow him even though he held one hand over his mouth as he spoke and when he smiled he did so with his mouth closed. This was because even when in the shape of a man, the creature still had the long, sharp canine teeth of a bear. And when that person who had been entranced by the monster's sweet voice had been led deep enough into the forest, then that awful being would suddenly turn and leap with an awful roar. All that would be left of that unfortunate victim would be bones that the monster bear would carry back to its lair. It piled up those bones and slept upon them as a bed.

The villagers had all heard the stories of this *otgont* bear creature, but had never encountered one—until now. Finally, the head clan mother spoke. Her voice was sad. "Now we know what has happened to our people who vanished," she said. "They have surely been devoured by that unclean being. But this is not the time to become lost in sorrow. We must do something and not just wait to be victims."

She looked around the circle of anxious faces.

"What can we do?" said the leader of the hunters. "If the stories about this creature are true, then its skin is too tough for our arrows or spears to pierce it. No weapon can kill it. If we go out to hunt it, it will just hunt us instead."

Suddenly a small voice spoke up.

"I have an idea," said that small voice. Everyone turned to look at the one who had said those words. It was the littlest boy in the village, the one almost everyone ignored. His parents had died and he lived with his aged grandmother in a little patched-up longhouse.

Although she loved her grandson, she was so old that her eyes were no longer good, so she did not notice that the boy's hair was never combed and that his face and clothes were never washed. In fact, his buckskin shirt and his blanket were full of holes. The name his parents had given him was Ahtondas, which means "Listener." But everyone in the village just called him by the nickname of Dirty Face, because of the way he looked.

One of the hunters laughed at the boy. "What do you know?" the hunter said. "You are just a little boy with ragged clothing."

Others joined in the laughter. But the laughter ended suddenly when the head clan mother held up her hand.

"Let the boy speak," she said. "I have seen how he sits by the fire listening when stories are told. Those holes in his clothing have come from the sparks that leap out from the fire. He listens so closely that he does not even brush those sparks away."

Little Dirty Face stood up and stepped forward. "I remember it being said in the stories that if someone challenges the monster bear to a race and wins, he may be able to destroy it."

The people looked around at each other

and nodded their heads. It was true. That was what more than one story said.

"Good," said the head clan mother. "This young one has spoken well. Now, who among us will be the one to race that creature?"

Once again there was a long silence. None of the men lifted their heads to speak up. Even the leader of the hunters stared down at his own moccasins.

"If no one else will do this," a little voice finally said, "then I will try to do it. I will challenge the monster bear."

It was, of course, Ahtondas, the boy everyone called Dirty Face. And this time no one laughed at him.

That boy went out and did as he said he would do. When the Bearwalker came to him in the shape of a man, he saw it for the monster it was. He challenged it and the race began. For four days he pursued it, making a fire each night and sitting with his back to the fire for safety. At last the Bearwalker could run no farther. It fell to the ground exhausted, right in front of the cave where the piled bones of its victims lay.

Ahtondas lifted up his bow to shoot the monster. As he did so, the Bearwalker laughed.

"Your arrow cannot kill me," it snarled up at

him. "My skin is too thick. Shoot it and then I will rise up and kill you and gnaw the flesh from your bones."

I imagine that boy standing there, his bow drawn back, his arrow pointed at the Bearwalker. The smell of death and decay comes out of that cave where the bones of the monster's victims lie piled in a great heap. The Bearwalker's teeth are long and sharp. Ahtondas can see the hunger in its eyes. But his hands do not shake.

"I know your weakness," Ahtondas says. "Your heart is hidden behind that white spot on your body."

Then he shoots his arrow.

That story I loved so much as a child has become all too real to me now. But I'm not the boy in that old story who could run forever without tiring. I don't have a bow and arrow. No weapons at all. And my own hands are shaking as I write this.

1

Pioneer Junior High

I hate the name of my school. Almost as much as I hate the fact that I am the shortest kid in eighth grade. There are even sixth graders taller than me.

But I am not small enough to be forgotten by at least one person as I slouch in my corner desk with my head down.

"Baron," Mr. Wilbur says from the door of the classroom. "Come on, buddy. Let's go. Everybody else is outside."

So much for my wonderful idea. I should have known it was too good to be true when the principal announced over the PA that any student who was not outside promptly at 9 A.M. and lined up for the bus would be left behind.

I shoulder my backpack and go out the front door of the school. I'm mad that my idea about getting out of this "special experience" hasn't worked. I don't notice that Mr. Wilbur has turned back to get something and is not behind me. Mistake number one. Mistake number two is walking out in the blinding sunlight without noticing what gang of three boys is hanging around the door. The three main reasons I am dreading the days ahead.

"Oops," says a familiar voice, just before a leg hits my shin at just the right place to send me sprawling onto my face. My hands scrape the pavement, but at least I don't hit my face and get a bloody nose like I did the first time this happened to me. One thing I've learned in the time I've been at Pioneer Junior High is how to fall.

I look up over my shoulder at the big round face of Asa Denham. His long blond hair is like a halo lit by the sun around his head, but his amused expression is not that of an attentive angel. His two buddies—who hang around him like the other two-thirds of a set of Siamese triplets—look over each of his shoulders. Ernie Crimmins and Harle Clark look just as self-satisfied as their leader. I don't know which one of the three tripped me, but they're all enjoying the spectacle of me flattened on the sidewalk like roadkill.

"Sorry," Asa says.

"Yeah," Ernie agrees. "Sorry you're such a clumsy little shrimp."

"Shrimp," Harle repeats. His imagination is limited.

Not surprisingly, seeing as how downed prey always attracts the pack, other kids have quickly gathered round.

"Fight?" someone says in a hopeful voice. As if I were about to get up just to get even more convincingly flattened.

"Yo," a foghorn tone chips in, "what happened to Baron? He trip over an ant?" It's Willy Donner, of course. Willy is a weird match for that big voice of his. He's as skinny as I am short. But he is always so quick with his sarcasm that no one ever gets a chance to make a crack about him before he makes some biting remark of his own.

Someone pushes his way in front, takes my arm and lifts me up.

"Come on, Baron," he says. It takes me a moment to realize who it is. I'd been expecting a teacher to be the one to step in, but it's not. It's Cody Campbell. Cody is not just one of the biggest, he's also the best-looking guy in the eighth grade. Sort of a teenage Brad Pitt. The girls swoon over him. And because he's the best football player in school, the guys all respect him, too. Asa and his crew have already taken a few steps backward to disappear into the crowd.

I'm still trying to get over my shock about Cody actually noticing me, much less lending a helping hand to me, when I hear the AP's brusque voice.

"Move aside," he snaps, as if he actually had to say something for the crowd to part before him like the waters of the Red Sea. No one ever wants to get on the wrong side of Assistant Principal Stark. He stares down at me as if trying to identify some lower form of life that just crawled out from under a rock.

"What's going on here, Mr. Braun?" he says. "Did I hear someone say 'fight'? Has someone been picking on you?" His hooded eyes take in the scrapes on my hands before I can put them behind my back. ZTP, I think. ZTP.

ZTP. That stands for the zero tolerance policy in effect at our school when it comes to fights. Anyone involved, including the hapless victim, gets punished. All I have to do is mention Asa's name and we'll both be up the creek. In detention, probably denied the opportunity to go on the class trip. Hmm. I'm tempted. But what works against my temptation is the ancient junior high code of Omerta. Nobody squeals on nobody, no matter what.

"I tripped," I say. "Mr. Campbell here just helped me up."

"Humph," the AP snorts. He turns on his heel and strides back into the building.

Cody slaps me once on the chest, a friendly slap that confuses me. It's as if I've done something admirable.

"You never cry, do you?" Someone else has come up next to me. It must be the Indian boy's day for having white kids sneak up on him. It's a girl this time. Her name is Tara and her desk is next to mine. She hands me a tissue. "Your hand is bleeding," she says. Instead of saying anything, I just press the tissue against the scrape on my hand and walk away from both of them.

As the class lines up for the bus, I look back at the redbrick buildings of the school. Could it really be six months since my uncle Jules dropped me off here for the first time?

He had volunteered that first day to pick me up from the trailer park and take me to school because Grama Kateri can't drive. I was in a bad mood and Uncle Jules was good at picking up that vibe. Unlike some adults, he didn't think the right thing to do was to tell me it was all going to work out for the best. He knew as well as I did that things didn't always work out that way. My mom might get blown up in an unarmored Humvee on the road to the Baghdad airport. Or just vanish like my dad did in Afghanistan two years ago. Uncle Jules had been a Marine himself back in World War II. Ours is a military family. Ancestors of mine have fought as U.S. soldiers, preferably Marines, in every American war from the Revolution up to the present day. Always as volunteers. Always in the front lines. There are more Purple Hearts in my family tree than branches.

I'm proud of that, but pride didn't make me any less depressed that day. I was upset about my mom going away again and having to farm me out with Grama Kateri. Not that I dislike my grandmother—she's great. But she's not my mom. And where my mom was going, I might not ever see her again.

To be honest, I was also upset about what I knew I was heading into. A whole new school where I'd have to make new friends (if I was lucky, which was unlikely) and avoid being stereotyped as a Native American midget (which was probably inevitable). So I was struggling between feeling worried about my mom and feeling sorry for myself, and being angry at her for deserting me and being angry at myself for being so selfish. Although I tried not to show it, my face probably looked like a battlefield that day.

A year is plenty of time to fit in, right? Like a square peg is going to fit into a round hole if you just give it time? You could say that when I arrived here in the middle of my seventh-grade year I settled into a well-defined niche that was purely my own and remains so in eighth grade. The niche of a minuscule, mouthy Mohawk misfit. And nothing is going to change that. Not even a trip to an Adirondack camp. No matter how much my teacher, Mr. Wilbur, tries to pump this up as a great adventure.

To be fair, Mr. Wilbur is a good guy. He's the first male teacher—aside from the phys ed teacher—I've ever had, and he loves books. He's in the school library as much as I am, and not just because he and our librarian, Ms. Mars, are friends.

Ms. Mars is your typical dedicated school librarian. She's always suggesting books like a literary marriage broker, wedding readers to the titles just right for them. She makes a special effort for the kids who are (and she says this with a little significant pause before the word) readers.

Which describes me. When I was in elementary school at the Akwesasne Mohawk School and stepped into the school library for the first time, I was the kid who said in a too-loud voice, "I'm gonna read every book in here!" That earned me a hug from Mrs. Smoke, the first librarian I ever fell in love with. It also earned me a beating from Billy Jacobs and Timothy Laughing after school. Even in an Indian school with other Indian kids, if you're little and call too much attention to yourself, you attract the bullies.

At Pioneer, the first book Ms. Mars handed me was *Freak the Mighty*. Which was okay. I liked the story and the way it was written, but I thought her motivation in suggesting it to me was a little transparent. When I brought it back to her and she asked me what I thought about it, I sort of wised off.

"It was okay." I shrugged. "What you got for me now? The biography of Tom Thumb?"

Her face got red. Then she turned around and walked away from the desk. "I'll be back," she said.

I felt bad as I stood there. But I still thought I'd made my point. If I were the only African American kid in the class, would she have recommended *Up from Slavery* to me? She headed for Mr. Wilbur. The two of them put their heads together and did some whispering. Then she went to a back shelf and pulled out a book. When she came back, she was no longer on the verge of tears. And what she had in her hands was something really special.

I have this thing about bears. It's not just that I'm a Mohawk Indian and I belong to the Bear Clan. It goes way beyond that. I've had a lifelong fascination with bears. Their gentleness and their strength has always touched something deep in me. My mom said my first word was *bear* and I had a stuffed one that I named Buddy. I carried Buddy with me everywhere, which wasn't that easy on him. Mom patched him up a million times until he finally completely fell apart when I was five. Then my mom and dad and I had a funeral for him just like he was a person.

I can't get enough of bears. I'm always reading about them. I draw pictures of them on my notebooks. I even have a bear paw design sort of tattooed into my left arm. I did it with a sharp pencil, poking it in and drawing blood with each stab. (I don't recommend you try that, seeing as how I got an infection that ended up making my arm swell like a balloon and I had a fever for two days.)

"Here," Ms. Mars said, holding the book out so that I could see the design on the cover.

I snatched the book so fast—like a grizzly grabbing a piece of raw meat—that I almost took Ms. Mars's fingers with it. I don't even recall walking out of the library. There was just me and the book. The rest of that day I spent every spare second (and most of math class) reading it. *The Sacred Paw: the Bear in Nature, Myth, and Literature.* I brought it back to the library the next day.

Ms. Mars looked surprised when I walked up to her desk. "Returning it already?" she said.

I shook my head. "Can I buy it?" I asked.

I couldn't, of course, but Ms. Mars got on the Internet and helped me locate a used copy on eBay for four bucks. When we completed the transaction I grinned up at her.

"This," I said, "could be the start of a beautiful friendship."

Mr. Wilbur also has picked up on my ursophilic fascination. One of the reasons I like him is because he lets me get away with a lot. I don't mean stuff like throwing spitballs or making rude hand gestures when his back is turned. Those things are adequately covered by Asa and his crew. I mean that he lets me turn just about every writing assignment into a treatise on bears. Like when we were doing poetry I used a poem from *The Sacred Paw* about "the heavy bear who goes with me." (Mr. Wilbur was amused that in my critique I talked about how using bears as metaphors would work better if the poet knew something about real bears.) When we did Shakespeare I wrote three whole pages on the stage direction "Exit, pursued by a Bear."

Mr. Wilson even aids and abets. Just last week he loaned me a book I hadn't seen before, *Touching Spirit Bear*. It's about how old-style American Indian circle justice was used on a non-Native kid who'd done a lot of bad stuff. Instead of sending him off to a juvie jail they exiled him to an island. There he ran into you know what. Eventually, after a lot of hard lessons, that kid learned to listen to his heart. I read the book in one sitting, read it again, and then returned it to him.

"You liked it," he said, smiling. He saw the look on my face.

"You bet," I replied. "Think we could arrange for Asa and his crew to get sent to that island?"

"Well," he said, rubbing his chin like he was actually considering it, "maybe not an island. But there is one way we'll be getting everyone outdoors this year."

Mr. Wilbur loves the outdoors. He's always saying things like "We need to attune our senses to the rhythms of the nature cycles." And his favorite word seems to be *listen*. He'll just stop in the middle of a lecture and say that.

"Listen."

Then we're all supposed to get quiet and listen. And some of us do eventually hear what it is he wants us to notice. Like maybe a cardinal calling from a branch just outside the open window of the classroom.

He's taken courses on things like animal tracking, making a fire with a bow drill, building survival shelters in the forest. Now, my being an Indian, you might imagine I would know about all that stuff. But most Indian kids, even those on the rez, are not learning those things anymore. They're too busy doing all the things other kids do—watching DVDs, playing Xbox games, and downloading rap music on their iPods. All that I knew about animal tracking was what I had read in books.

And the only real bears I've ever been close to are the ones I saw in the Syracuse zoo. My mom drove six hours to take me there the week before she got shipped out. I didn't want to see the elephants or the snakes or anything else. We spent the whole time with the bears. Most people just walked past because the bears weren't doing anything much except lying there. But I didn't care. I just wanted to be close to them and feel their presence. I felt as if I were in there with them, looking out of their eyes, sharing their thoughts. My mom only suggested moving on once. When I didn't answer, she sat down and put her arm around me. We stayed until one of the zoo people came and said we had to leave.

"So soon?" I said.

"Son," the man said in a gentle voice, "was up to me, I'd let you stay all night. But we got rules here and we done bent 'em some already. It's an hour past closing time."

But he didn't make us get up and go just yet. Instead he sat down and talked with me about the bears, how he liked taking care of them, though he'd rather see them out in the wild since there was always so much going on in a bear's head and life had to be awful boring for them in their enclosure. That was why he gave them balls to play with and hid their food so they had to spend time figuring out where it was.

It was dark when he finally led us to the back gate and let us out.

Before we left, though, he tapped me on the shoulder.

"You might want this," he said. He was holding a wooden carving of a bear. It was about the most beautiful, perfect little thing I'd ever seen. Not a cartoony bear, but like a real animal shrunk down, every detail just right.

"I can keep it?" I said as he placed it in my outstretched palm.

"Well, maybe it can keep you," he said with a big grin. "Bears bring you luck, you know."

"Thank you, Roy," my mother said.

Our car was the only one left in the lot. It didn't hit me until Mom pressed the button on her key chain to open the doors.

"Roy?" I asked.

"He served with your dad in Afghanistan," my mother replied. Her voice was so soft I barely heard it.

I didn't say anything after that. I just kept

my hand in my jacket pocket, holding on tight to that little bear. We pulled out onto the road and I guess I fell asleep then because I didn't wake up until hours later, when my mother opened the door to reach in and slide her arms under me. She hadn't picked me up like that since I was in second grade, and I suppose I might have protested that a mom just doesn't carry her seventh-grade son, even if he is still only knee high to a gopher. But I didn't. I just leaned my head against her shoulder and felt her strong arms—strong enough to carry the whole world—holding me safe and secure as she took me up to bed.

That year-ago drive to Syracuse with my mom was the last trip I'd really wanted to take until now. And now, whether I want to or not, I am about to get on this bus for the annual eighth-grade trip to Camp Chuckamuck. Four nights in a wilderness camp to do some of those same things that Mr. Wilbur learned. I sigh as I climb the steps. Maybe I'll really like it after all. I mean, how bad could it be? All I have to worry about is more of the usual junior high bullying I've been suffering the last six months. It's not like my life is going to be in danger.

trees

The miles are whipping by. We've gone from flat farmland to rolling hills. The once-distant peaks of the Adirondacks have edged closer. They're tinged with the colors of autumn, that blood red of the maples and the yellow of the beeches flowing like colored patterns in a tapestry across the green unchanging fabric of the spruce and pines and cedars. Whiteface Mountain rises up like a volcanic peak above the others. I'm actually feeling pumped.

The thought of being among all those trees, big ones that I can get way up into, is making me feel happy as I look at those mountains that are growing larger and larger. I practically live in that big maple that grows out over the street behind Grama Kateri's trailer. I think nothing about dangling out by one hand over the road for minutes at a time from my favorite high branch.

Mom climbed plenty of trees when she was my age. And I imagine that was true for Grama Kateri as well. After all, they were once bear cubs just like me. Among our nation, you inherit your clan from your mother's side. Grama Kateri and Mom are both Bears. My dad, being Turtle Clan, stayed out of trees.

Maybe I'll find a hundred-foot pine to climb. I've read that a few old pines in the Adirondack Park are almost as big as the ones that grew before the English and French took the tallest trees to make the masts of sailing ships.

"ENTERING ADIRONDACK PARK."

I read that sign by the roadside aloud. It prompts Mr. Wilbur to say something in reply. He's just come back to his seat next to me after quelling some minor disturbance in the back of the bus.

"You know we won't actually be in the park itself," he says. "Camp Chuckamuck is on private land just outside the Blue Line."

"It is?" I hadn't known that.

Mr. Wilbur hears the disappointment in my voice.

"Don't worry," he reassures me. "It's just as wild at Chuckamuck as anywhere inside the park. It was a family preserve before it became a camp and they kept it pristine. It's still that way, despite the pressure being put on the owners to sell it to developers. Plus it's way off the beaten track. You'll see when we get to the road that leads in. Ten miles of dirt! You're more likely to view megafauna here than anywhere else in the North Country. Moose and even. . ." He pauses for effect and then just makes a growling sound.

"Bears," I say. I'm grinning now.

Mr. Wilbur starts to say something else, but the sudden dramatic rise of a voice from behind us drowns out his words.

"All they found of that one kid was his hand. And all the fingers had been chewed off!"

I don't even have to turn around to know who it is. Willy Donner, of course. His foghorn tones reverberate through the whole bus. He's three rows back, trying to freak out the girls in the seat across from him with stories about the cannibal of Camp Chuckamuck.

"His name," Willy continues, pausing and lowering his voice for dramatic effect, "was Jason Jones. His parents brought him to Camp Chuckamuck twenty years ago. He was huge for his age, but he wasn't really smart. The other kids teased him and played mean tricks. What they didn't know was that they were driving him crazy and that he was wicked strong. One night, after they put a dead rat in his bed, he just ran screaming out into the night and never came back. No one could find him. But the next night the boy who had put the rat into Jason Jones's bed vanished. A trail of blood led from his cabin into the woods."

I take a quick look over my shoulder. Heidi and Tara, the two Willy's words are aimed at, have disinterested looks on their faces. But they're still listening as he gruesomely chronicles how one camper after another disappeared.

"They started finding things around the camp. There were piles of eyeballs that had been pulled out and human leg bones with tooth marks on them."

Willy's voice gets louder again. He's approaching the climax. "The state police finally tracked Jason Jones down to a cave in the forest. That cave was piled high with chewed human bones and there was a big iron pot in which he was cooking up a batch of camper soup. Even though the police shot him again and again, he wouldn't die. He just kept coming at them until they finally had to use a flamethrower."

I look over at Mr. Wilbur, who is rolling his eyes like I am. Like flamethrowers are standard issue for state troopers? Talk about overembellishing.

"But before he died, engulfed in flames," Willy concludes, "the last words Jason Jones howled were 'I'll be back.'"

Mr. Wilbur has his head in his hands. Like me, he doesn't know whether to laugh or cry. Although I have to admit that some of the details of that story have creeped me out.

But Willy isn't done yet. He leans toward Heidi and Tara, his voice a harsh whisper: "Every year the ghost of Jason Jones, the cannibal of Camp Chuckamuck, comes back to claim another victim. And this time it might just be . . . YOU!" As he shouts that last word, Willy grabs Heidi by the arm and she screams.

Mr. Wilbur stands up and turns around. He doesn't do it quickly, but he has a presence that makes people pay attention to him, whether in the classroom or on this bus full of overstimulated teenagers. He speaks just one word. Firmly.

"Enough."

Willy sinks back into his seat and directs his eyes forward. Heidi, who enjoys acting hysterical, stops screaming, even though she is still rubbing her wrist where Willy grabbed her. Tara, too cool to fall for Willy's tale of terror, just shakes her head in disgust.

Mr. Wilbur slides back into his seat in one easy athletic motion. He was a gymnast in college. He's the only teacher I have ever met who can do a backflip.

"Urban myths," he says. "Well, actually rural."

"An unconvincing mélange of overworked motifs," I add, putting on my best professorial voice.

Mr. Wilbur chuckles and holds up his right hand to tick them off on his fingers. "*I Know What You Did Last Summer,*" he begins.

"*Friday the 13th,*" I add.

"*Halloween,*" he continues, shaking his head. "Poor Jamie Lee Curtis."

"With a little touch of *The Terminator,*" I conclude.

"I'll be baachh," Mr. Wilbur intones, nailing the Austrian cyborg accent.

Three seats back, Willy is talking again. Mr. Wilbur sighs but doesn't do anything. You can't keep a bad storyteller down. At least Willy is soft-pedaling it below foghorn level now. I can still hear him though.

"You know," Willy says, "Camp Chucka-muck was built on an old Indian graveyard."

Now I roll my eyes. It always comes back to that. Every spooky place in America, it seems, was built on an old Indian graveyard. I'm as sick of hearing that as I am of being told that the only real Indians live west of the Mississippi. But Willy isn't finished yet.

"You know what the word *Chuckamuck* really means?" he asks. "It means place of many chewed bones!"

Now I'm ready to stand up, but Mr. Wilbur holds out his hand. I settle back in my seat. I understand. It's not the time or place to get into this. All I'd be doing would be knocking my head against the wall. What Mr. Wilbur expects is that after a few days together here at the camp, things will change. We will learn in spite of our-selves, inspired (as the camp brochure reads) "by the healthy outdoor atmosphere and the natural environment of Camp Chuckamuck, whose name means Place of Happy Meetings in the language of the first peoples of this land."

I think it's a faint hope. People don't change overnight, even in a healthy outdoor atmo-sphere. The bus bumps and sways into a turn. I look out the window. We've just turned onto that dirt road Mr. Wilbur mentioned. Hills crowd in on either side, and evergreen trees are thick all around us. It's almost like we're going into a tunnel that leads to another reality.

Thinking of reality, *Chuckamuck* is not a word that means "Place of Happy Meetings" in the Mohawk language. In Mohawk it doesn't mean anything. That's par for the course when it comes to most outdoor education places. They like to use phony Indian names. Either they spell them wrong or don't translate them right or they just plain make up some weird word that they think sounds Native American.

I'm feeling sort of depressed now, despite the trees and the chance of seeing a bear. Too many things are going through my head, especially that image of Jason Jones's cannibal cave full of bones. I know the yarn that Willy was spinning is just a crock. But it's made me think of another tale, one that really is old and traditional. There *was* a real cave full of chewed human bones in the story of the monster bear.

3

First Sight

"Yo, Mr. Wilbur, are those real?"

"Check it out!"

"Look at that!"

Thirty-three other Pioneer Junior High eighth graders stare out the windows as our bus slows down. We're creeping over a wooden bridge that spans a swampy forest meadow and deepens into a pond created by a long beaver dam. The dam is about fifty yards back from the road and it's a miracle of animal engineering. It has to be a hundred yards long. But that intricately fashioned wall of mud and peeled sticks is not what's attracting my eyes or those of the other kids. Some of them are holding up their cell phones to take pictures of the center of all our attentions. It's our first sight of creatures we've been told about but have never seen before.

"There she goes again!"

The cow moose that is three times as big as any white-tailed deer lowers her head once more into the pond. She raises her head and water streams off her. A braid of water weeds hangs like a beard from her jaw as she chews the plants she's foraged from the bottom. She seems oblivious to the presence and noise of our passing. Behind her, in shallower water, her two calves stare over their shoulders at our bus.

For a moment I feel as if it can't get better than this. We haven't even gone a mile yet off the main road and we've already experienced something I've only imagined or seen in pictures. Those big animals seem like beings out of the past. I feel as if I'm no longer in the twenty-first century, but in a time where the old stories are alive.

Then the sarcastic voices of Asa and Ernie and Harle jolt me back into the present.

"Man, if I only had a gun."

"How about an RPG?"

"Yeah, that'd do it. Ka-boom! Course all you'd have left would be the head."

They're laughing like hyenas now. They've reduced this moment of awe to an adolescent fantasy of animal slaughter. I hunch into myself. I know that the Turtle is my dad's clan and not my own, but at moments like this I find myself wishing I had a shell. I could just pull my head in and pretend the rest of the world—which can be so mean—doesn't exist.

I'm alone in the seat. Mr. Wilbur stood up and moved back along the aisle when the three moose first came into sight. He's telling the kids what he knows about moose, how they've come back into the state after being absent for so many years. It wasn't just that they'd all been killed by hunters. The disappearance of the northern forests eliminated their habitat. But now the woods have been growing back for more than a century. With forests to return to, moose have been slowly spreading west from Maine into New Hampshire, Vermont, and now the Adirondacks.

How does he do it? He's actually managed to quiet Asa and his clique with his soft-spoken lecture. He's up to the challenge of handling thirty-four eighth graders on a bus where he and the driver are the only grown-ups. The other adults coming to Camp Chuckamuck with us are in the smaller van with all the camping gear. Three parents and Mrs. Smiler, the girls' PE teacher. They fell behind when they had to stop for gas.

Mr. Wilbur drops back into his half of the seat again.

"Don't," he says. Then he waits.

"Don't what?" I finally reply.

"Take a guess."

"Don't let those guys get to me when they are being jerks?"

"Bingo."

"That's easy for you to say. You're a six-foot-tall adult teacher."

There's a longer silence this time. I'm looking out the window, but except for an occasional chipmunk or red squirrel taking its life into its paws to scurry across the road in front of the bus, there's no sign of any other animals.

"I suppose I could tell you," Mr. Wilbur says, his voice slow and careful, "that kids who are bullies and loudmouths are that way because they don't feel good about themselves. You know, a person is not born a bully."

"So it's not like my situation, eh?" I answer. I always have an answer when I'm in this kind of mood. "Not like being born the runt of the litter."

"Baron," Mr. Wilbur says, directing my gaze out the window, "look up."

I do as he says. We've entered another cleared

area, an old decking ground for logging where the trees were cut back and a hillside is exposed. You can see the sky over that hill and there, even though it is early afternoon, is the full moon. It is just hanging there, luminescent in the west, almost as visible as it would be at night. Full moons in the autumn can be like that. Even though the sun is lower in the southern sky, the moon is still high, reflecting the sun, giving a second chance at the light. Mohawks call the moon Grandmother. We say that she watches over us when she is big and full that way.

"You don't have to be tall to see the moon," Mr. Wilbur says.

I don't argue with that.

We go around one curve, dive down into a valley, and climb a steep grade. There's a small building, more of a shack than anything else, by the side of the road where some machinery is parked. Small as that building is, it has a huge padlock on its solid door. keep out and stay away are painted in large red letters on the three sides of the shack visible as we bump past. What's being kept in there?

Just past that mysterious shack the road

abruptly narrows. It's just wide enough for our bus as it passes between two steep rocky hills. Another mile or so and we come out of the gap. Now I can see the blue of water glinting ahead of us. We turn again and then we're there.

When you come to a new place, pay attention. That's one of the things my dad and mom have often told me. Part of it is from their military training and part of it is just the old Mohawk way. So I look around slowly, taking it all in. First there's the pond. It's nothing like the pond where we saw the moose. This one is bigger, clearly man-made, with a concrete dam wedged like an open palm between two small hills to hold back the water of the two streams that flow down the mountain into it. It's as neat as a picture postcard. It's been edged with white sand. There's a swimming float in the middle and a dock with a dozen boats tied to it.

Then there are the buildings. The first one we pass, which is at the start of a trail that rises quickly up the mountain to our left, is a small frame building with a porch. It looks lived in and the clothesline out back is a sure sign of that. A couple of small red-and-black patterned shirts and several pairs of wool socks are hanging from the line. As we continue to follow the road around the pond I count the rest of the buildings. There are six and they're all log cabins, like out of a travel brochure or a corny old movie.

Several people are ranged around the biggest one, a square-built florid-faced blond man. He has one of those "I'm in charge" smiles on his face. Ten to one, he's the camp director. He and the two others with him wear khaki uniforms with little triangle-shaped designs stenciled on the left pockets, yellow ball caps with that same triangle, and identical blue-and-white sneakers. Their welcoming grins look as manufactured as their clothing. Clones.

I amend my first impression when I notice the older-looking couple standing a little off to the side. They look like real human beings. They both have deeply tanned faces. The woman wears a floral pattern dress like those Grama Kateri favors. The man holds a pipe in one hand and a splitting ax in the other. His clothes look like larger versions of the ones I saw hanging on that line. The square-built blond man notices them just then. He turns and waves a hand at them in a dismissive gesture and they disappear back around the building.

Two medium-sized single-story cabins lie

to each side of that main building, rustic signs on their log walls. CHICKADEE JUNCTION, GIRLS' BUNKHOUSE. Cornier than Iowa. But the boys' bunkhouse is worse. HAWK HAVEN, it reads. Hawk Haven? No haven for me if all the boys will be staying together there. I have no doubt that Asa and his crew of apprentice sadists will be tormenting me with unfunny practical jokes. Rather than a place of refuge, that boys' bunkhouse is where I fully expect that my life will be made into a living . . .

"Baron?"

I wake up from my vision of inevitable torture. Everyone else has gotten off the bus. I'm the last one left sitting inside. Surprisingly, the person who has just stepped back in and spoken my name to return me to the real but no less bitter world is not Mr. Wilbur but Tara Moody. She touches my arm lightly and smiles.

"Come on, dreamer," she says, looking down at me with a little smile. "You're in my flight."

Flights. It's been explained that we'll be broken up into groups called flights. Why? Because Camp Chuckamuck "gives wings to the spirits of every child." To which I want to reply, "Give me a break instead." Or maybe just remind them that I'm a bear, not a bat or a bobolink.

However, I am so surprised by Tara's unexpected friendliness that my protective armor of sarcasm falls away. I get up out of my seat, smile up at her (she is a good foot taller than me), and follow her off the bus.

But as soon as I set foot on the ground and see the huge man who seems to have appeared out of nowhere, I freeze in my tracks. He's leaning back against the main camp building, the sign EAGLE'S NEST half obscured by his broad shoulders. A chill runs down my back.

terrible Creatures

've always had this ambiguous feeling about scary stories, whether they're modern ones like that overblown tale of Jason Jones that Willy was spinning or ancient stories from the time of my ancestors. Whenever my mom or dad would ask me if I'd like to hear a story, part of me would be eagerly saying yes while another part of me was just as vehemently saying no. I knew that the nighttime tale they'd tell might have a monster in it.

Mohawk stories have the world's scariest monsters. Long ago, the forests were full of bloodthirsty things stalking the night. Hungry giants with skins made of stone, huge panthers with eyes of fire, whirlwind creatures screaming through the air, ogres that were once just greedy humans—until they ate their own flesh and then became cannibals with an insatiable lust for human prey.

There were so many terrible creatures in the old days, it's a wonder that any of my ancestors escaped to pass the stories on down. I asked my parents that very question.

"How did any of our old people survive?"

Mom nodded in appreciation of the wisdom of my question. I was only eight years old then.

"Hmm," she said. "I can think of two reasons. One is that our old Mohawk people were tough."

Dad chuckled at that remark. "Especially the women," he said. That earned him a punch in the arm from my mother.

"See what I mean, my son," Dad said, cradling his arm as if it was broken. "Our women are daaaan-gerous."

Mom shook her head, but she couldn't keep from laughing. It always made me feel safe and secure when they teased each other like that. I miss that feeling—and both of them—so much.

"What's the second reason, Mom?" I asked.

I had to do that. It looked as if they were about to get into one of their full-scale wrestling matches. They just did it for fun, but when both your parents are soldiers with black belts in karate, a kid learns when he needs to keep a discussion focused.

My mom raised one eyebrow at my dad. "Later," she said, cartoon menace in her voice.

"I can't wait," Dad replied. "Bring it on."

"Bad parents! Behave!" I said. They both laughed at that, but it worked.

Mom settled back down with her arm around me. "The second reason," she said, "why our old people survived, even surrounded by all those terrible, hungry creatures, is that we've always been smarter."

If you were smart enough, if you just used common sense and the lessons taught you by your elders, you might be able to defeat a monster. Even if you were a little kid. I liked that. That's why I kept listening to the stories they told and asking them for more. Those scary stories made me feel safe. Safe because my big strong parents were there with me. Safe because every story they told always came to an end. Safe because the hero or heroine of the story usually found a way to defeat whatever threatened the people.

Usually. But not always. If you were stupid or selfish, if you didn't show proper respect to the natural world, the monster might just win. That was always there in every story. There might still be a happy ending, but not for the foolish human in that tale.

Why did my parents tell me those stories? I ask myself that question a lot these days now that they're no longer with me. I'm as alone as one of those long-ago orphan boys who had no one to care for him but his old, weak grandmother. (Although no one better call Grama Kateri weak if they want to remain unbruised!) I suppose my dad answered that question that day when I was eight.

"It still must have been scary back when there were monsters," I said.

My dad leaned over and put both his hands on my shoulders. "Son," he said, "it's still scary now."

Standing here at the foot of the bus steps, trying not to stare at the tall figure who hasn't seemed to notice me yet, I'm hearing my dad's voice say those words.

There's no logical explanation for the way I'm feeling. But I sense something very wrong about the one I'm looking at from the corner of my eye. You don't make eye contact with a predator unless you're prepared to attract its attention.

Activity is swirling around me. The man in charge of the camp, the square-built blond guy with the sunny smile so broad it must make his face hurt, is talking with Mr. Wilbur and the other adults whose van pulled in while I was sitting in the bus. Things are being unloaded, people are talking, there's an occasional shriek from one of the girls—usually Heidi. Every now and then someone jostles by me. Everyone is doing something. Everyone except me and . . . him.

He's wearing the same khaki shirt as the others, with that triangle camp logo on the shirt pocket, but that is where all resemblance to the other staff ends. You might say that he looks like an Indian. He has long black hair down to his shoulders and his complexion is almost as dark as mine. Porcupine quill earrings dangle from his earlobes and he wears a leather band around his forehead. There are Indian bracelets on both his wrists, turquoise rings on his thick fingers. Instead of sneakers he wears moccasins on his feet. A big silver Navajo belt buckle is at his waist. His necklace is made of huge bear claws.

That necklace sends a shiver down my back. I know how much some folks, some Indians included, like to wear jewelry decorated with animal claws. There was a time when I thought about wearing a bear claw necklace, it being my clan animal. But after what Grama Kateri told me a few years ago, I decided that I would never make or put on a bear claw necklace of any kind.

"Some people," she said in a sad voice, "hunt bears just to chop off their paws and pull their teeth for making necklaces and cut out their gallbladders to make a kind of medicine. They just leave the rest of the bear to rot in the woods."

Even if I were a person who made necklaces out of grizzly bear claws—and there are some of our people who do that with prayer and care and respect—I know I wouldn't make one like the one he is wearing. His necklace is more than just the claws, which haven't been cleaned but have pale dried flesh there and look like they were roughly torn from the bear's paws with pliers. The bones that the claws were attached to are also on that necklace. It makes me think of one of our tales in which the monster wears a necklace of shrunken human skulls. Or the more modern story I heard on TV about soldiers overseas who cut the fingers off the enemies they killed and strung them together to wear around their necks.

The one wearing that grisly necklace might look Indian to some, but I don't think he is. You can't always tell if someone is Indian by the color of their hair or how they dress. Over the years our people adopted in plenty of folks from other tribes: Abenakis, Mohegans, Irish, English. I once saw a painting in the cultural center up at Akwesasne that was done by a Tuscarora artist, Rick Hill. It made me smile and then nod my head in recognition. It showed an old-time Mohawk man with a roach-style haircut, his face all painted, his clothes those worn three hundred years ago. But his hair was blond, his facial coloring fair. The picture was titled *The First Blue-Eyed Mohawk*.

It's not just hair and skin and clothing. There's a way people hold themselves and talk and behave that makes it clear who they really are, what nation they hold in their hearts. There's something about that one there that freaks me out. His hair, the way he's dressed, everything about him seems unreal. Like it's all a disguise. He's pretending to be something that he is not. Not just pretending to be Indian. Pretending . . . to be human.

He's studying the crowd of us. Watching us the way a mountain lion might eye a herd of deer from a place of concealment. I'm so short that I don't think he can see me. Then he suddenly turns his head. His eyes catch mine; I can't look away. A little smile curls his lips.

"I am doomed!" someone behind me declares. "My life is over!"

I quickly turn my head away to look behind me.

It's Willy Donner. He's holding his cell phone and frantically tapping away at its keys. He holds it up again. "Look," he says, his voice as tragic as that of a shipwrecked sailor. "No signal!"

"Cell phones do not work here," a know-it-all voice intones. "No towers in these mountains." It's the square-built man in the khaki uniform. He's close enough now for me to make out the name tag on his chest.

MR. MACK, CAMP DIRECTOR, it reads.

"So you won't mind handing them over," Mr. Wilbur adds. He has a box full of manila envelopes in his hand. "Write your name on the envelope, put the cell phone into it, seal the envelope, and hand it back." He pauses and holds up his finger. "Also any other electronic devices. IPods, Game Boys, whatever. You are all officially now unplugged."

Mr. Mack and his assistant counselors go around collecting the electronic devices. There's a lot of them. Enough bulging envelopes to fill a big cardboard letter file box. There's some grumbling, of course, but everyone gives up their gadgets except for me. I just don't own any of that stuff, especially not a cell phone. Grama Kateri firmly believes they cause brain cancer. Mom agrees with her. So there's no one I'd be calling on one.

While the electronic toys are being collected, I sneak a wary glance back toward the EAGLE'S NEST sign. There's no longer anyone leaning against the wall. How could someone vanish that fast? Was he just a figment of my overactive imagination? But even if he wasn't real, in the conventional sense of things, I am certain that I had a vision of something threatening.

5

Journal time

I'm sitting in my bunk now. We have an hour for journal time. *Find a quiet place. Write down your impressions of your camping experience thus far.* The boys' cabin is about as quiet as it can get because no one else is in here. That is muy cool by me.

You might think I'd be out exploring the woods, looking for signs of animals, communing with nature. After all, I'm an Indian. Isn't that what we are supposed to do? Not. I try to avoid those stereotypes about Native Americans that the other kids and even some of my teachers seem to have. I never wear any Indian jewelry or moccasins. (You can bet I have never mentioned the regalia stored at Grama Kateri's that I used to wear when Mom took me to dance at powwows.) I keep my hair short—a Marine-style haircut. I can't do anything about my skin color or my features, but most non-Indians don't see you as a real Indian unless you're dressed for the part. Sneak under the radar. Fade into the background as much as possible.

Even so, under other circumstances, I really would have been out in the forest like a shot as soon as I was given the chance. Stereotypes be danged. But things are different now. I have some real reasons for caution.

I got tripped again as soon as I stepped through the door of Hawk Haven. Being little is an advantage in one way, though. When someone trips you, you don't have far to fall. I went right into a roll that brought me back up to my feet again. Mom had taught me that, as well as making sure when you roll that you come up facing whoever has just tripped you. Asa, of course. He didn't press what he might have thought was his advantage. Maybe my rolling up to my feet surprised him. Maybe the way I was holding my hands up like a boxer deterred him. Or maybe he remembered that Mr. Wilbur and the camp director, Mr. Mack, were just outside.

He and his crew did have one other little surprise for me. The twelve bunk beds ranged around three walls of the cabin came supplied

with thin foam mattresses. Twenty-four mattresses. More than enough for seventeen boys.
Except Asa and his boys grabbed all of the seven
extras. That left no mattresses on the remaining
bunks. I would have had to spread out my
sleeping bag on bedsprings—if they even let me
claim a bunk for my own.

I figured none of the boys would risk their
necks by speaking up for me. When a wilde-
beest is being chewed on by a pride of lions, the
rest of the herd just looks the other way in
relief. My only recourse would be to complain
to the adults, which would make me even more
contemptible in everyone's eyes as a squealer. I'd
rather sleep on the floor.

I was surprised, though, at what happened
next.

"Hey, Baron."

It was Cody. He hooked a thumb toward
the bed directly over. As I stared in disbelief, he
pulled off the extra mattress he'd placed on his
bed and flipped it back over his shoulder onto
that top bunk, his eyes on Asa and the others the
whole time. Asa's jaw dropped so far I thought
he'd bruise it on the floor.

Somehow I'd found, if not a friend, at least
someone who was not going to treat me like

pond scum. Under most other circumstances I would have been feeling optimistic about my chances of continued survival were it not for my new major reason for worry. A reason I could only hope was just my imagination.

I should talk to someone about this, but there's really no one here I trust enough. The adults, even Mr. Wilbur, would say I was being silly. All I trust is this journal—my secret one. I've already finished writing something safe and nonrevealing—about how exciting it was to see those three moose—in my school journal. That's the one that Mr. Wilbur will see. No mention in it of bullies or fearsome, possibly illusory figures.

I've spent too much time covering up my real feelings, any obvious signs of weakness or loss, to start sharing my fears with anyone outside my family.

Dad and Mom both told me that the surest way to get mugged when you are walking down a dark street late at night in a big city is to give off fear vibes. Act like you think you're going to be a victim, you end up as one.

"Of course," Dad had added, "the smartest thing to do is to avoid being alone on a dark street late at night in the first place."

I'm taking Dad's advice now, trying to avoid trouble. Here in this upper bunk in the corner with my back to the wall I can at least see anything that might be coming at me. I'm not off alone in the woods where something huge and deadly might be lurking behind any big tree or bush or rock.

But I can't stay here forever. I look at my watch just as I hear the clanging sound of a big cowbell being hit by a stick. It's the signal for everyone to gather in the main hall. We're going to rejoin our flights—back to the flock. Time to work together, build teams. Happy little birds, be solitary sparrows no longer.

We'll meet the rest of the camp staff and then be told what group task we have to accomplish for the two remaining hours before dinner—maybe nest-building. Dinner will be our first meal in the dining hall. We were all given lunch bags from the school cafeteria when we left Pioneer Junior High, which we ate on the bus. A sour apple and two peanut butter sandwiches are lodged in my gut like little gooey fists.

I slide my pen into the rings of my private journal and stick it down into the deep breast pocket of my shirt. Slinging my back pack over my shoulder, I climb slowly down the ladder. Why hurry when every step just brings you that much closer to your doom?

Bear Facts

Journal time has come and gone. We've all gathered together to listen to Mr. Mack lecture us about what he calls—with a little insincere laugh—"the bear facts."

His voice is monotonous but I'm listening close, making sure he has his facts right.

"There was a time," he says, consulting the magazine he holds in his hand, "when *Ursus Americanus*, the American black bear, was almost gone from this land. Here in the Northeast, two hundred years ago, almost all of the forests where bears lived had been cut and turned into farmland. Not only that, bounties were being paid on such large carnivores as bears, wolves, and mountain lions."

I have to nod my head at that. It's true. In the early 1800s they were paying five dollars a head for bear scalps, which was big money back then. There was a war on bears.

It wasn't just that those animals sometimes killed livestock. People were afraid of them. All kinds of grisly stories were told about humans being killed by wild animals . . . or saved from them at the very last minute by a hunter who was just in time to shoot the bear or wolf or mountain lion as it was about to pounce on some innocent person. Kind of like that woodsman who rescues Little Red Riding Hood from the evil wolf.

In point of fact, though, it was those big animals that had to be afraid. For every wolf or bear or mountain lion that even looked at a human being, thousands were killed. There's nothing more dangerous than humans.

"In all of the North American continent," Mr. Mack continues, turning a page, "over the last hundred years, only fifty-two humans have been killed by black bears—most of them people foolish enough to get in between a mother bear and her cubs or unlucky enough to come upon a bear that had broken into a camp for food. What a bear does then is try to get away. And if you are between that bear and the door, you'll be moved aside by that frightened but potentially lethal bruin.

"Today the bears have returned. Slim as it

may be, there's always the chance of a dangerous bear encounter when you are in the northeastern forests nowadays. In the Northeast, from Maine through Pennsylvania, it's been estimated that there are now as many as fifty thousand wild bears."

It's a canned lecture. I know all of those facts, even though they're new to most of the other kids with me. Some of the kids in our group had begun voicing their fears about running into a bear even before they got off the bus here at Camp Chuckamuck. Or maybe *fears* is not a strong enough word. Try *near hysteria*.

It seems that even though I was the only one who stayed in my cabin during the journal time an hour ago, none of the other kids ventured into the woods at all. It was starting to get dark, so they all just hung around within sight of each other and the main camp building. And when someone—and wouldn't you know it had to be Willy Donner—saw something fairly big and black walking around behind the main cabin, he raised the alarm in that stentorian voice of his. People started screaming (boys as well as girls, I might add) and running.

"Bear! Bear!"

"It's after me!"

"Help, a bear is chasing us."

Those terrified shouts had brought me outside just as fast as everyone ran for shelter. A real bear? Cool! I was actually hoping to see it.

Instead, I arrived on the scene just in time for the camp cook's rotund black Labrador retriever to waddle up to me and lick my face.

Apparently my classmates' reaction to wild bears is par for the course. Especially after newly arriving campers see the warnings posted in every building about what to do if you see a bear. This lecture Mr. Mack is giving was originally supposed to be part of the orientation talk after dinner.

He lifts up the magazine he's been getting his facts from. "It says," he reads, "that for every person killed by a black bear, 45 are killed by dogs, 249 by lightning, and 60,000 by fellow human beings." He looks up and gives us a big insincere grin. "See. Nothing to worry about. It says that black bears are actually very shy. If you see a bear in the wild, don't run. Just back away from it quietly, or shout and stomp your feet." He closes the magazine and looks around at the still-worried faces of most of my classmates.

So do I. I can't believe it. Am I the only one

who's not a chicken? Even Asa and his crew, who've always tried to make everyone think they are so fearless, were quaking in their boots at the sight of a chubby canine. Some of them would probably still have been trying to crawl under the tables if I hadn't called out, "Hey, guys, it's just a dog."

I reach down and pat Poe-boy, the dog curled up at my feet, on his broad head. Poe-boy. He's the black Labrador that started the mass panic and now seems to have adopted me as a new friend. With the blessing of his owners. Mrs. Osgood, the woman in the flowered dress I'd seen on the porch when we arrived, had quickly figured out what was happening. She came right out to claim her dog when she heard the screams for help.

We had struck up a conversation while I was petting her dog and the counselors were rounding up the rest of our group who had scattered like a flock of hens fleeing from a fox—taking refuge in the main hall, the bunkhouses, the latrines, and in Asa's case, on top of the bus. I learned two things about Mrs. Osgood right away. One, that she and her husband were Indians themselves. Abenaki. The second was that punctuation meant nothing once she started a sentence.

"Nice to see that you've taken a shine to our dog our boy Fred was like that when he was your age and your size though he is all grown up and gone away and I was just thinking of him today when I was airing out to give to the Salvation Army some of his old clothes you might have seen on the line back of our cabin where there's just the three of us now, me and George and Poe-boy, our dog here, and I named him that because there was this one poem I always liked called 'The Raven' which was about a black bird and seeing as how Labradors is often raven black and the man what wrote the poem was named Poe and that Poe-boy is a male dog . . ."

You get the picture.

The only thing that stopped her flow of words was the arrival of her husband. I liked Mr. Osgood as soon as I saw him. He was as thin as his wife was round. He had that tough, weathered look that some Mohawk elders have—like he was made of sinew and leather. He wasn't dressed in modern clothing, but wore red and black wool pants held up by suspenders and a work shirt with a similarly patterned wool coat over the top. In those clothes he looked like a lumberjack or an old-time guide. A little like my uncle Jules, in fact. Uncle Jules always favors clothes made of natural materials like wool and cotton. Even when they're wet, he says, they keep you warm. Not like these new space-age fabrics.

Mr. Osgood's long gray hair came down to the shoulders of that old wool coat. It framed a narrow face seamed with smile lines. In his left hand he was holding a stick connected by a string to an old cast-iron frying pan he held in his right hand.

"George," Mrs. Osgood said, "put down the bear pan and come meet these two nice boys Baron and his friend Cody who have made friends with our Poe-boy and . . ."

"Any bear come into camp," Mr. Osgood said, "they just hightail it for the hills when we bang on this bear pan. Even faster than your fellow campers done when they thought a bear was after 'em."

Mr. Osgood looked down at me with a twinkle in his eyes. "Aren't you afeared of bears, young fella?"

"No sir," I said. "I'd like to see one."

"Hmm." Mr. Osgood nodded, a pleased look on his face. "Some spare time, I ought to take you and your friend here up to the Bear Seat."

I look over at Cody, who is sitting on the other side of the fire during Mr. Mack's speech. I have to give him credit. Although at first he ran inside the boys' cabin, he was also the only one who came back and stood next to the door to try to guard it—with a broom that he picked up, no less—just in case that black beast tried to follow them in. As a result, he saw that the supposed bear was nothing but a dog and came over to join me petting Poe-boy.

Cody senses my eyes on him. He looks my way and actually smiles. He's still a little embarrassed at having been spooked, but is able to see the humor in the way he and everybody else acted. My mom always told me you can trust folks who know how to laugh at themselves. Cody's smile encourages me and I relax. Maybe too much.

"Any questions?" Mr. Mack says.

I raise my hand. It's as if there is another part of me taking over and I'm not really sure what it is about to say. And what is worse, I can't seem to stop it from happening. It's like when a stone breaks loose from a hillside and starts to roll. Nothing is going to halt it until it hits the bottom.

"Yes, ah . . ."

"Baron," I say. "My family is Mohawk. I grew up hearing stories about black bears. None of our people were ever afraid of real bears. We even have a story about how a mother bear took in an orphan boy and cared for him like she was one of her cubs."

Why am I saying this? Is it something in the air here? After a year of semisuccessfully allowing my Indian ancestry to fade into the background, I have just blown my cover bigtime. Clam up, dummy! I tell myself.

I manage to snap my mouth shut before I babble out anything else that might be used against me later. It's probably too late. I can already imagine Asa war-whooping at me and his buddies sarcastically calling me "Little Bear."

Mr. Mack is smiling even broader, but his eyes don't look happy. I get the feeling he's not that pleased that I spoke up.

"Baron, thank you. How wonderful. I'd love to hear that story." He looks around the circle. "And I am sure that everyone else here feels exactly the same. An authentic Native American traditional tale! Perhaps we can convince you to share it with us around the campfire one of these evenings."

Or perhaps you could convince me to shoot myself right now, I think.

There's no way it can get worse than this.

Stories About Bears

Wherever you go, Indians have stories about bears. And bears are a lot like people. They walk on two legs at times and when a bear is skinned it looks like a naked human being. Bears eat some of the same food that people do. They even have the same illnesses. The strongest of the old medicines among my own Mohawk people were supposed to have been given to us by the bears. People watched what bears ate when they had certain sicknesses because they found that eating those same medicinal plants would make people get better, too.

My dad and mom once took me to the Six Nations Indian Museum in the little northern Adirondack town of Onchiota. It's on the other side of the mountains from where we are, over to the northwest near Saranac Lake. It's one of the old-style Indian museums, not like one of those big new ones funded with casino money. The Six Nations Museum was built by a Mohawk elder named Ray Fadden, constructed by him and his relatives with their own hands. It's a big old log cabin, in the shape of the long-house. It's only open in the summer because it doesn't have modern heating or air-conditioning. Its only "climate control" is a woodstove. Simple as it is, though, it's full of information about the history and culture of our Iroquois people. The walls and even the ceiling beams are hung with so many things—posters and wampum belts, gustowehs (the traditional feathered cap our men wear), moccasins, cloth-ing of all kinds—that you feel dizzy trying to take it all in.

Ray Fadden had been a teacher at Akwesasne back when my dad and mom's par-ents were young people. In fact, he taught all four of my grandparents. He was their favorite teacher because he passed on so much about our old ways at a time when everyone else was turning away from our traditions. Finally he quit teaching and built the museum to keep on sharing those old ways with the new genera-tions. Being taken to his museum by my mom and dad was kind of a family tradition, even though Mr. Fadden himself, who was in his nineties by the time I went there, was living in an elder care center up on the reservation.

The best part about the place for me was the stories that Mr. Fadden's son, Kahionhes, told us. He'd been an art teacher in the Saranac Lake schools but he was now retired and had taken on his father's job of keeping the museum open in the summers. Some of those stories were very old—but the ones I liked best were the ones about his dad and the animals, especially the bears.

Food had become scarce for the birds and animals because of the acid rain in the Adirondacks, so for years and years, Ray Fadden provided food for the animals in the woods he owned all around the museum. He would buy birdseed and had an arrangement with the markets to pick up their food scraps. Sometimes as many as thirty black bears would come to the big rock back in the woods where he placed food for them.

He never fed them by hand or followed them around or tried to make them into pets. He respected them too much for that. But he sort of learned how to talk their language. There are all kinds of vocalizations that bears use. Like, there is a growl a bear makes to warn you to keep away. And when a bear is greeting you in a friendly way it kind of sways its head back and forth and makes a kind of *unnh-unnh, unnnhh-unnhhh* sound. A little smile came over Kahionhes's face as he told us how whenever his father met a bear in the woods he would do that—bend over and sway back and forth and go "Unnhh-unnh, unnnhh-unnhhh"—and the bear would do it back to him. Then they would each go their own way. Bears also hoot to each other—just like owls.

There are some sounds that can mean you're in danger. The first is a deep cough that is a threat. "Get away from me or else" is what it means. And then there is actually a sort of whistling, chirping sound that a mother bear uses when she is calling her cubs. You need to walk away from that sound, too. The worst place anyone can be is between a mother bear and her cubs.

Kahionhes took us out behind his father's house and pointed out the big rock where the bears came to eat. So much fat had soaked into it over the years that it shone in the sun like it was made of glass. But we stayed way back from it because it was the bears' place and not ours.

And we didn't see any bears that day.

Mom and Dad promised me they would take me back to the Six Nations Indian Museum again. But that autumn my dad was sent to Afghanistan and never came back. And then the summer after that Mom did her first tour in Iraq. So most of what I have learned about bears since then has been from books and TV shows on the Animal Planet channel.

"You can learn a lot from books," my dad said to me. "Just remember that books are like people."

Dad was always saying things like that. He didn't elaborate about what he meant, but I think I understand. Just like people, books don't have all the answers. They can be right or wrong, honest or dishonest. But you can always learn something from both people and books—even those that try to deceive you, as long as you figure out that is what they're trying to do.

One of the things I learned from books that I believe to be true is that in the right way of things, the bears walk their way and we humans walk ours. When someone joins the bears, it is only because things are not right with the world. Like in that story I mentioned to Mr. Mack. When a child is lost, the bears may take that child in for a while. But the right way for the story to end is for the child to go back to being a human, carrying with them what they've learned from their stay among the bears. But if someone who is a grown-up strays into the territory of the bears, then the results will not be good. Death may be what follows.

Bearwalkers. That is what the Ojibway people who live near the Great Lakes call those who choose to put on the skin of the bear, to gain power in that way—and be corrupted by that power in turn. When you become both a human and a bear, your double heart no longer sees the light as either humans or bears do. It was from a book that I learned that to become a bearwalker you have to sacrifice one of your own family. Blood for power. And then power calling for more blood.

All of that has gone through my mind as Mr. Mack keeps talking. Then he turns his gaze toward the back of the crowd and makes a wide gesture with his hand. Sort of like a ringmaster about to bring in the lion tamer.

"Now let me introduce a very important member of our staff. He's been off setting up the primitive camping area so you have not met him yet. He's new to us this year, but he brings a very special kind of knowledge our way. He's our wilderness expert. The one who will be taking you into the woods and"—Mr. Mack chuckles as he makes what he thinks is a sly little joke—"bringing most of you back again. Our own Native American tracker, Walker White Bear."

Everyone else applauds. I don't. I don't even want to look back, but I do. And there, stepping out of the woods behind us, is the one I knew I'd see. The grisly necklace that he wears looks as if each bear claw is tipped with blood.

8

Bad Vibe

I lean my head back against the rough bark that still clings to the log siding on the wall of the boys' cabin. I've been assigned to fire-tending detail, but I've slipped away from it. It's only an hour until dark, and it's the kind of darkness that comes earlier, more suddenly, more completely here in the forest. There's no gradual fading into twilight like there is in the lake-plain lands. Just one second it's day and then the next second it's deep night.

I should be bringing more wood to make sure there is enough for the fire to keep burning all night. There's electricity in the cabins, but when nine o'clock comes it is supposed to be lights out. Total darkness inside. And aside from the lights that are kept on in the two latrines and in front of the main building—lights that I know will look pitifully small—the only illumination outside will be from the campfire. There's a full moon tonight but it was increasingly cloudy this afternoon, so even those ancient beings of light that show their faces through the blanket of night probably won't be looking down on us.

But I'm not getting wood. For one reason, the person who is in charge of the fire scares me even more now that I've actually heard what he had to say. Hair stands up on the back of my neck when I remember the sound of his voice. It spooked me even more when I looked around and saw that his voice was clearly not having that effect on everyone else. To them it sounded the way he wanted it to sound. Deep, reassuring, helpful, informative.

"Pay attention now, young people," he rumbled. "Watch how I'm holding this knife while I make this fire stick. There's a right way and a wrong way. Right way—cut away. Wrong tack—draw it back. You never want to cut toward yourself unless you are fixing to slice the skin off your finger for a little snack. Hunh-hunh!"

And everyone laughed with him at that joke about cutting his own flesh. Well, almost everyone. They even laughed when he pretended to do just that—slice a piece of flesh off his finger.

• • •

I was waiting now to try to talk with the one person who had looked skeptical as Walker White Bear gave his little demonstration about fire-making. That person was engaged in a serious discussion around the corner from where I was standing. My aim was not to eavesdrop, but sometimes you just can't help hitting what you aren't aiming for.

"You might be overreacting, Kirk," Mrs. Smiler says. "You only met the dude two hours ago."

"Listen, Ginny," Mr. Wilbur says. I can picture him stroking his chin with his fingers as he says it. "There is something wrong here."

"A bad vibe?" Mrs. Smiler replies. I can tell by her tone that she is being sarcastic. When she is teasing someone she likes to resort to sixties lingo, even though she grew up in the nineties. She'll say things like "You're tripping me out, man" when a kid complains that PE class is too hard or "Right on" when someone manages to do something like a forward roll correctly.

"This isn't a joke," Mr. Wilbur says. I'm not used to hearing him sound so serious. "And yes, I am getting a bad vibe about this whole trip. Why would they hire someone like him? After the first five minutes of his lecture you could see he didn't know squat about fire-making. And it's not just . . . him. I didn't know the entire staff of the camp had changed. The only people who were here before are the cook and the caretaker."

"So you don't like Mr. Mack, either?"

"Now that you mention it, no. I'd like to see his résumé. Does he act or talk like someone who's used to working with adolescents? And did you see the way he treats the Osgoods? They've been here for over twenty years and he acts like they're just peons. And what was up with him just reading from a magazine and pretending it was a lecture about bears? And all that talk about what kind of injuries bears can inflict on a person? It was like he was trying to either bore them or frighten them to death. There's something fishy going on."

"Then why haven't there been any complaints from other school groups coming here?" Mrs. Smiler asks. She's not joking now. Mr. Wilbur's words seem to be getting through to her.

"Listen," Mr. Wilbur says. "We're the first group to come through this fall. Don't you remember? Camp Chuckamuck was closed for the last two months of the summer. But did you know that it wasn't even certain it would ever open again?"

Of course I've been listening, but now I pay more attention as Mr. Wilbur explains how Mr. and Mrs. Philo, whose family founded the camp two generations ago, just decided this past year they were too old to run it any longer. He'd had a heart attack and she had bad arthritis. They'd immediately been offered a huge amount of money for their fifteen hundred acres by developers. People were interested in buying luxury condos in the wilderness and because the camp was not inside the boundaries of the Adirondack Park, development was not restricted by the Adirondack Park Agency. Chuckamuck was less than an hour's drive from the Adirondack Northway, a four-lane highway that led to Montreal in one direction and New York City in the other. Chuckamuck was also less than a half-hour away from some of the prime skiing areas in New York. The state of New York had also been trying to obtain the land to add it to the forest preserve. It was only a short time ago that the decision had been made not to sell—at least for now. The Philos were less interested in money than in preserving their beloved camp for young people. They had no living children of their own—their own kids had died in an accident. Their only heirs were two nephews. So the plan now was to not sell it to either the state or the developers. Instead, they were putting the whole camp into a conservation easement to make it possible for more generations of kids to come here.

That was what Mr. Wilbur explained. And that he knew all this background information because the Philos, the people who own the camp, are longtime friends of his own parents.

Mrs. Smiler has been listening without making a peep through that whole long explanation. But from the sound of her voice when she finally does speak up, she seems unimpressed.

"So it's a win–win situation for the kids and the founders of the camp. Groovy. What's the hassle?"

I hear Mr. Wilbur sigh, then take a deep breath. "Listen," he says. "The papers haven't been signed yet. What if this whole camping season is a disaster? What if they decide not to put it into an easement and it ends up being sold to developers? You know who would benefit financially? Those nephews. And I'd be willing to bet they're the ones who hired this rinky-dink staff."

"Kirk," Mrs. Smiler replies, "I still think you're being paranoid. Get real."

I wait until the sound of her feet walking away on the gravel is gone. Then I go around the corner to where Mr. Wilbur is still standing.

"Baron," he says, dropping his hand from his chin and trying to lose the worried look on his face. "What's up?"

More than you know, I think. More than you know.

9

Unexpected Arrivals

'm not exactly sure what I am going to say to Mr. Wilbur. I'm not one of those people who makes up speeches in his head, trying to get every word just right before speaking up. But when I do get started, I usually say exactly what is on my mind. This is another reason why my mouth has gotten me into trouble in the past.

But I don't get a chance.

A horn honks from behind me and I almost jump out of my skin. Even though a part of my brain has been registering the sound of wheels rumbling along the dirt road, I've been so intent on talking to Mr. Wilbur that I've ignored it.

There's a big smile on Mr. Wilbur's face as he looks over my shoulder.

"Wally and Dora," he says. "I can't believe it! I never expected them to be here."

An old blue Ford Bronco in mint condition

is pulling up. There's a handicapped parking sticker in the window. An elderly woman with a huge halo of white hair is the driver. She waves one hand at us as she climbs out, then slowly begins to make her way around to the other side, where an equally elderly man in the passenger seat is waiting for her to open the door.

"Come with me, Baron. I want you to meet just the people I need to talk to right now."

We trot over to the car in time for me to get the door and for Mr. Wilbur to offer his left arm to the tall, thin old man who is now slowly climbing out as well as hug the elderly woman with his right.

"Kirk," the elderly man is saying, "I'm not an invalid. I can get out by myself." But I notice that he doesn't push Mr. Wilbur away as he says this and that he leans his weight onto my teacher as he brings one foot and then another down onto the ground with the careful deliberation of a heron wading into uncertain waters. I reach out my hand to help him balance and he takes it. His hand is dry and cool and his long fingers wrap around my wrist. It doesn't bother me at all. I'm used to helping old people like that. I do it all the time with Grama Kateri on the days when her "rumatiz" is acting up.

"Thank you, boy," the cloud-haired old woman says, patting me on the back. "So nice to see a young man with manners." Then she pokes a finger at the chest of the old man. "Not an invalid, you say? Hah. Let's you and me run a hundred-yard dash and see who wins now, Wally Philo."

She turns to look down at me.

"Boy," she says, "Wally's walker is in the backseat. Be a dear now and get it before this old fool falls down on his face and we have to use a derrick to get him back up again."

As I go to the back door, Mr. Philo raises his hand in a gesture like that of a priest about to give a benediction. "Fall down? Hah. With this new wiring in my chest, by this time next week I'll be dunking a basketball again."

"In your dreams, darling," Mrs. Philo replies.

"If I could interrupt for a moment," Mr. Wilbur says, "let me introduce one of my students to you. Baron Braun, these two superannuated cutups are the founders of this camp, Wallace and Dora Philo."

Mrs. Philo reaches over to grasp my hand. "Braun? We knew a Braun family, didn't we,

Wally? You a Mohawk, boy?"

"Yes, ma'am," I say.

"*Seh'kon*," Mr. Philo says, leaning over to take my other hand with those long fingers of his.

"*Seh'kon*," his wife repeats.

I'm stunned. They've just greeted me in flawlessly pronounced Mohawk.

Mr. Philo is the one who explains. "I was a fairly successful professional basketball player. Way long ago."

"Before the invention of the wheel," Mrs. Philo interjects.

"Along the way, I learned how popular basketball is among Indians. So I used to do a workshop every now and then in reservation schools. That's where I picked up a bit of Mohawk. I remember back about twenty years ago there was a tall young man by the name of Braun who had some promise as a guard at the Akwesasne school."

"That would be my dad," I answer. I wait for them to ask the question I don't want to hear. Where is he now? But they don't ask. The Philos just look at each other and nod.

The four of us stand there in silence. It isn't awkward, more like the kind of silence I'm used to experiencing around Indian elders, a silence that gives folks a chance to just settle in with each other. Mr. Wilbur is the one who finally breaks it.

"I have to say I'm really glad to see you both. This is perfect timing. But what brought you here?"

For the first time, the Philos look surprised.

"Are you joking, dear?" Mrs. Philo says. "You're the one who left us the urgent message saying that we had to be here at Chuckamuck today."

Mr. Wilbur puts his hand to his chin. "Listen," he said, "I didn't send you any message at all. I wonder what—"

He doesn't finish that sentence. The sound of an explosion cuts him off.

Stuck

The road is totally blocked. Unless we want to walk, we're stuck at Camp Chuckamuck. We're gathered after dinner around the big fireplace in the main building. Almost all of us are here except Mr. Osgood. Just about everyone is acting like all of this is no big deal.

But I don't think so. This is a *big* deal. That explosion didn't just block the road, it also took out the phone lines, which ran between the hills that collapsed when the dynamite went off. The only reason we still have electricity is because the power company strung their lines over the hill rather than through that gap.

Poe-boy bumps his wide flat head against my arm. He looks up at me with his big, sympathetic Labrador eyes. It's like he's trying to tell me something. I reach out and rub his head and neck and his tail thumps on the floor in response. Before he left, Mr. Osgood told him to stay, even though he whimpered and struggled so much to follow him at first that he had to be shut in the kitchen. It was like he knew it wasn't safe for his master to go off like that on his own. It was only after Mr. Osgood had been gone for half an hour and he stopped scratching at the door that Mrs. Osgood finally let him out.

The explosion had surprised just about everyone, except the Philos, who knew what it was right away.

"That was your dynamite, dear," Mrs. Philo had said in an admonitory voice to her husband while the blast was still echoing over the lake and people were running around like chickens with their heads cut off.

Mr. Philo's dynamite, as his wife kept calling it, was indeed what caused the explosion. That shack with the KEEP OUT and STAY AWAY warnings painted on its side had been built by a professional contractor to store the explosives that were supposed to have been used to widen that narrow gap between the rocky hills. Mr. Philo's heart attack a year ago had stopped that construction project, though. What surprised the Philos was that the dynamite was still there. It was supposed to have been removed because dynamite can become unstable if it isn't stored properly.

"We'll be having a word with that contractor," Mr. Philo said to the crowd of campers gathered in the main building, who had become an appreciative audience for him and his wife.

"More likely a number of words we won't repeat in polite company," Mrs. Philo added. Just about everyone laughed.

I didn't. I was worrying about too many things. The dynamite shed was so close to that gap in the hills that when it blew, it brought down tons and tons of stone as well as the trees that were growing higher up. Halfway through the gap the road just ended in a twenty-foot-tall wall of stone and earth, topped with toppled cedars. On either side of those hills the land rose into mountains. There was a walking trail that swung around the now closed gap and rejoined the road. But even an off-trail vehicle wouldn't be able to negotiate that. The only way around the landslide was on foot.

Other trails, of course, led out of Camp Chuckamuck. They were all hiking paths or old overgrown logging roads that snowmobilers used in the winter months. You couldn't get a car or a truck down any of them. And the shortest of those trails was twenty miles around the mountain with two rivers to cross before reaching the nearest town.

No one was supposed to be coming in to Chuckamuck until our bus driver returned to pick us up. But that was not scheduled for another three days. We were stuck until then unless someone did something.

"Well," Mr. Osgood had said when the road situation had been explained to everyone, "I appear to have been elected."

As the camp caretaker, he saw it as his job to go out and make contact with those who could bring in earthmoving equipment and open the road again. With dozers and a backhoe, it would take no more than a day or two. The idea of a long walk didn't bother him at all.

"Ten miles is naught but a random scoot," he said. "But I do not expect to have to hoof it that far." He reached into the pocket of his green wool jacket and pulled out a spark plug. "I'll just pop this into Matilda and ride in style."

Matilda was Mr. Osgood's all-terrain vehicle, a four-wheeler that he kept parked under a tarp a mile down the road past the now vaporized explosives shed. Keeping Matilda spark-plugless was his way of ensuring no one else took her for a joy ride.

His wife handed him the backpack that he called his "old kit bag." It contained a thermos, a sandwich, and a flashlight.

"All I need aside from Betsy," he said, tapping the stock of the old single-shot .22 rifle that was slung over his left shoulder.

I wish I could have stopped him. But what could I have said or done? What did I know besides the fact that I had awful feelings of impending doom?

And what can I say now as everyone sits here after dinner, relaxed and listening to Mr. and Mrs. Philo tell their stories? Even Asa and his crew are enjoying it. So much that they seem to have completely forgotten about making my life miserable. As if.

Mr. Wilbur looks over at me, nods, and gives me a big thumbs-up. He's noticed that Tara is sitting right next to me here in the corner on the floor. Somehow she seems to have adopted me as her little pet. She even keeps nudging me now and then, peering over my shoulder to see what I'm writing in my notebook. But I cover it with my hand whenever she does that.

"Aren't the Philos just the sweetest?" she whispers in my ear. "Are you writing down their stories?"

"Just writing," I whisper back. I have to say something. For whatever reason—pity, maybe—she is being nice to me and it does feel good to have her leaning against me like this.

I straighten my shoulders. I have to think. I have to keep my eyes and ears open. Everybody else believes that it's all under control here. That the road being blocked is the worst that can happen. I just know it isn't.

I look up to scan the room. I've chosen this place in the corner not because it's close to the front where Mr. and Mrs. Philo have now moved from talking about the history of Chuckamuck to telling Adirondack tall tales. I've chosen it because from here I can see the whole room. I can see who is here and also who is not here.

And it is the thought of that one who is not here, the one I haven't seen since shortly after the explosion went off, that fills me with dread.

Where is he? That is one of the two questions that keeps running through my head. The other is, Why am I the only one who is worried? For a while, before the Philos got here, it seemed as if Mr. Wilbur shared my uncertainty. But when Mr. and Mrs. Philo arrived he got all relaxed. In fact, he now seems as happy as a clam in its shell. Even though they are just two frail old people, Mr. Wilbur seems to think their being here will make everything turn out right.

I guess I shouldn't be surprised. I sat at the same table where he and the Philos were talking during dinner and got the picture that they were like family to him. When he was my age he'd come to Camp Chuckamuck as a scared, self-conscious eighth grader and whatever they had done had given him self-confidence and courage. Being back in their presence made him feel like that little boy again being protected by the two people he trusted more than any others.

I appreciated that. Even though she was old (but not as old as Mrs. Philo), Grama Kateri sort of does that for me when I am around her. When you know that someone loves you and has faith in you, it changes things. It doesn't take away the pain of losing people you love—or make you grow two feet taller overnight—but it does make you feel less alone.

However, it ought not to make you feel so secure that you lose sight of what is really happening around you. Mr. Wilbur was the one who said that something wasn't right with these people who came to replace the Philos as the camp staff. Wasn't he the one who was trying to convince Mrs. Smiler how incompetent they seemed? Didn't he seem to think that the one they call Walker White Bear seemed really strange? He was the one who said how much money the camp property was worth if it was sold. Didn't he hear the Philos say that they came here because he invited them? Except he didn't—so who did? He seems to have forgotten about that mystery. And what about the road being closed by that supposedly accidental dynamite blast that also cut the phone lines? I've been asking myself those questions nonstop for the last few hours and gradually it has all come together, like the pieces of a puzzle. Can't Mr. Wilbur put two and two together? It all makes sense to me—too much sense.

I look at my journal, where I've written it all down. It adds up to even more than four. It adds up to the fact that we are all in terrible danger and that we are trapped.

I've been trying to get Mr. Wilbur alone to talk to him since before the Philos arrived. I stare hard at him, trying to get his attention. It doesn't work. He's sitting up front, his eyes on Mr. and Mrs. Philo, a little smile on his lips. Totally engrossed in their stories. So is Mrs. Smiler and the three parent chaperones who've seated themselves around the back of the room to keep an eye on any potentially restless students.

But the only restless student is me. Where is he? What is he planning to do?

"Where's who?" Tara whispers to me and I realize that I've been talking out loud to myself. Fortunately in a mumble, but loud enough for her to hear. She's trying to look again at what I've been writing in my secret journal.

"Nobody," I whisper back. A little too loudly. A few heads turn in our direction, but then are drawn just as quickly back to the front where Mr. Philo is talking about the really cold winter they once had here at Camp Chuckamuck.

"It was so cold," he says with a straight face, "that when we tried to talk while we were outside, our words froze in a cloud around our mouths. We had to pry those frozen words off, lug them back in, and thaw them out on the stove."

"That was the only way," Mrs. Philo chirps,

right on cue, "that we could carry on a conversation."

People start laughing, but Tara isn't giving up. "Who are you talking about?" she insists, poking me in my shoulder again. A part of me notices that she is doing that in just about the same way Mrs. Philo is now jabbing her finger at her husband up front. "Tell me or you are in big trouble, buster," Tara says, shaking a fist in front of my face in a mock threat.

I close my journal and slip it into the deep front pocket of my shirt. I shouldn't answer her. But her good-natured teasing unnerves me. I'm not used to a girl paying attention to me, especially one I have always secretly liked. The next thing I know, I hear myself answering her question.

"The one they called Walker White Bear," I say quietly.

"Oh," Tara whispers back. "Him. Didn't you hear them say that since Mr. Osgood was gone, Mr. White Bear was the one in charge of splitting the wood and then keeping the big campfire going back in the woods till it's time for us to gather there? That's where he is now. He's probably sitting out there in the woods by the fire now, waiting for us to finish in here and then come outside."

I should have figured it out. Despite the road being closed and the phones being out, we are going to go right back to our original schedule. Which includes a walk through the dark woods to the primitive gathering area and storytelling around the campfire.

Tara hugs herself and rocks back a little. "This is all so exciting, isn't it, Baron?"

I don't answer her this time. I feel as if there is a big cold stone in my stomach.

He's waiting outside for us. And like foolish rabbits hopping into a mountain lion's den, we are all about to go out there to him.

11

Lights

"You can never have enough flashlights." That is what Grama Kateri said as she helped me get my things together for the trip to Chuckamuck. Was it just last night when she said that? Was it just this morning when she hugged me good-bye and I walked out the door of her trailer and heard its rattly aluminum door bang shut? Right now it feels as if it were weeks ago, or even in another lifetime. So much has happened in only eleven hours.

But I am feeling very glad right now that she said those words, which were accompanied by her handing me a big plastic bag from the Double Discount Store. It held six flashlights of varying shapes and sizes and the batteries to go with them. One of them, a mini Maglite, has a band with a Velcro strip so I can put it around my forehead like a miner's light. That small light is in my left coat pocket, its weight balanced against the two cigarette-lighter-sized disposable flashlights in my right pocket. Two others, both medium-sized ones, are in my hip pockets. The black one is just a flashlight, but the red one has a laser pointer and a panic alarm in it.

The last and biggest of my six flashlights, which is eighteen inches long and as heavy as a club, is in my right hand. It has some kind of high-intensity bulb in it. When I turned it on as I stepped out of the meeting hall, it shot out a beam like a searchlight as I pointed it toward the cloudy sky.

"Whoa, Baron," Mr. Wilbur said. "Turn that off, buddy. If those clouds weren't up there you'd be blinding the astronauts in the international space station."

So I turned it off.

"If you turn your flashlight on while we are around the campfire, it will be confiscated," Mr. Mack had then announced, smiling all the time. And he had kept smiling as, one after another, he had taken away the flashlights that had been flicked on by various campers who were either forgetful or testing the boundaries. Each flashlight had gone into the canvas bag behind the log where Mr. Mack sat. Finally, by my estimation, I

was the only kid left with a flashlight. I could feel Mr. Mack just waiting to swoop down on me. No way. I was not about to have my light taken away, even if it did have to remain turned off.

But I'm glad to have the solid feel of it in my hand, especially since the only visible illumination here is the campfire. The last light pole of the camp is back at the trailhead, which is around a little hill that cuts off the fire circle from sight of the buildings of Camp Chuckamuck.

I'd feel better if my club flashlight were a gun of some kind. Preferably loaded with silver bullets. But the only gun in the whole of Camp Chuckamuck is Mr. Osgood's old .22, and it's not even here now because he took it with him.

Mr. Philo has finished telling the story he was asked to share to start out the campfire gathering. I've been listening pretty close to it because it is one of my favorites and the very one I mentioned earlier. It's the Mohawk tale of the boy who lived with the bears. The boy's parents had died and the only one left to care for him was his uncle. But his uncle had a twisted mind and resented having to care for the boy. So he took him deep into the forest, tricked him into crawling into a cave, wedged a stone into its mouth to trap him there, and then left. The animals of the forest rescued the boy, and because he was an orphan they offered to adopt him and allowed him to choose which animal family he would join. He chose the bears.

Mr. Philo's voice isn't the voice of an old man. It's rich and deep, and he tells the story so well that I forget there's anyone telling it. It's as if the story is just happening around me, as if I'm that boy safe in the security of the mother bear's protective presence. It makes me remember what it was like when my family was strong and whole, when both my mom and my dad were there with their arms around me.

I'm so close to the fire that it seems as if sweat is getting into my eyes, rolling down my cheeks. I wipe my face on my sleeve. I don't want anyone to think that I'm crying. It's just sweat, that's all.

Mr. Philo finishes the story. Mr. Mack stands up and starts slapping his hands together. That huge pasted-on smile is back on his face. "Everyone!" he shouts. "Come on! Show your appreciation. Let's all have a round of applause for the former director."

Everyone applauds, even though it breaks

the mood. Which is what I think Mr. Mack intended. Then there is an awkward silence. Using the heavy wooden cane that he leaned on as we walked to the fire circle, Mr. Philo has lowered himself slowly down onto the bench next to his wife. She's wrapping her blanket around his shoulders. He looks tired now. Mrs. Philo is whispering something into his ear and he is nodding wearily.

"I have a story to share," a heavy voice growls from the darkness behind Mr. Mack.

12

Real Stories

Mr. Mack is standing up and clapping his hands. "Wonderful!" he gushes. "Now we are going to hear a *real* Native American story from a true Native American."

My fear is overcome, for the moment at least, by my disgust at this obnoxious man and the disrespect he has just shown to Mr. Philo with that one simple statement. As if the story he just shared with us was a lie.

I don't know anything about how boards work, but I wonder how the board of directors for Camp Chuckamuck ever chose Mr. Mack.

Walker White Bear looms up from the darkness behind the camp director. He moves slowly as he takes the place of Mr. Philo on the slightly raised ground that elevates him above the rest of the circle. He's not as tall as the old basketball star, but he's a very big man. There's menace in the way he walks, each step so heavy that it seems as if his feet are sinking into the ground. I shove my hand into my pocket and find the shape of my bear good luck charm. It's just a carved piece of wood and I know I'm not being logical. But all I can think is that I need help. Just feeling it in my hand reassures me. A little.

"There's nothing as dangerous as a bear," Walker White Bear begins. His voice comes from so deep in his chest that each word is like the thud of a drum. "They're all teeth and claws. They'll tear you apart if they get ahold of you, and rip your head off. I've been around bears. I've walked with bears. Never show any weakness to a bear. Stand your ground. Face them down. Comes to the point where it's either kill or be killed, you have to be ready to do what needs to be done."

He looks around the circle of awed adolescent faces staring up at him. He has just about everyone here hypnotized. Not the Philos, though. And not Mr. Wilbur, who is sitting between the two old people with his arms around them. And not me.

The one who calls himself Walker White Bear nods his head and smiles a closemouthed, self-satisfied smile.

"Don't expect any favors from a bear. Whatever you get from a bear, you got to take." He reaches up one pawlike hand to grab the ugly claw necklace around his neck and shake it. "That story about a bear taking care of a child? Hrrrggghh!" His deep growling laugh shakes the air. "That's not going to happen. You know what a bear would do to a child? Let me tell you what I saw when I was up in Alaska, up where they have real bears and not those measly little black bears you get around here. Up where they have grizzlies."

He pauses for dramatic effect. I know that whatever he says next is going to be unpleasant.

"I was walking along a trail when I saw a little baby bear. It was up on a rock with its eyes closed. If any of you girls saw it you would have said it looked like a little teddy bear."

He slowly growls those words "little teddy bear" to make the mockery in his tone even more emphatic.

"Isn't that cute? You probably would have wanted to give it a hug. But when I got closer, it wasn't that cute to see. The whole lower half of its body was gone. One of those big bears had got hold of it."

"Sweet!" a voice interjects. I don't have to

look to recognize the voice as Asa's. I want to tell him to shut up, but I hold my tongue. I don't want to attract the attention of that big menacing, looming figure, have him realize how clearly I can see through the untruths that began with his very first statement.

"Sweet," Walker White Bear growls, nodding his head with pleasure as he repeats what Asa said. "That's just the way a little baby bear tastes. A big old male bear will kill and cannibalize any bear cub it can get its claws on. Why, even a mama bear will eat her own little ones if she gets hungry enough. Kill or be killed. Eat or get eaten. That's the real way of the world."

Walker White Bear pauses. I hope he's done, but I'm wrong. He spreads his arms wide. Some of the kids closest to him shrink back at that gesture, which makes it look for a moment as if he is going to grab someone, but he turns it into a yawn and a stretch. His mouth opens a little wider than usual and for the briefest second I catch a glimpse of his eyeteeth before he puts his hand over his mouth to cover them. They're not huge like those of a bear, but they are noticeably larger and sharper than most human canines. A shiver goes down my back. I look quickly down to avoid eye contact with him. I feel his inquiring gaze turned my way. The hairs on the back of my neck are standing up. Finally he looks away and starts talking again.

"But that's not the story I want to share with you. I know how much young folk love scary stories. And this is a story about this camp right here. A camp cook who was here over the summer brought her son with her. He was a big boy. He was quiet and seemed a little slow. The boys and girls who were here as campers were all from goood families . . ."

He drawls out those words sarcastically— ". . . good families"—making it clear that he means just the opposite.

"Those boys and girls had been given everything they needed by their rich parents. They weren't poor like the Joneses and their boy. But those spoiled little rich brats decided to torment that poor boy. They played mean tricks on him. They never figured they would be getting their comeuppance. Daddy and Mommy would always protect them. But then one day one of their tricks went a little too far and . . ."

"Stop right there!"

The tone of that voice is so commanding that Walker White Bear actually does stop. He turns, though, with a murderous look on his face to stare down at the one who just spoke up and who rises to her feet now, unafraid, to face him. It's Mrs. Philo.

"No!" she says. "You will not tell that story. What happened to that boy at this camp was a tragedy. I will not abide it being turned into a grisly tale to terrify young people."

Mr. Philo stands up by his wife. He may be a very old man, but his demeanor is not that of a gentle elder right now. He shifts his cane to his left hand as he holds up his right, his index finger raised toward the sky.

"Sir," he says, lifting the heavy cane to point it at the hulking figure's chest. "You're done." Mr. Philo's voice is not loud or filled with growling menace like that of the one he has just silenced, but there is such quiet authority, such dignity in his words, that everyone hears him.

Walker White Bear doesn't step back at first, though. He rocks onto the balls of his feet, almost like a bear about to charge. But the tall old man stands his ground, holding up that heavy cane as straight as a spear.

"Now," he says, gesturing to the side with his finger. "Go."

Walker White Bear turns away. For a moment it seems as if he is about to drop down on all fours. But instead he just walks out of the circle of light from the dying campfire and disappears into the darkness.

"I think we've had enough stories for the night."

It's Mr. Wilbur. He's standing next to the Philos. I hadn't seen him get up to join them. Everyone in the circle begins to move. Most people seem either a little confused or else oblivious to what has just gone on.

Mrs. Smiler leads the group back down the trail toward the turn around the hill where the first power pole will become visible. The use of flashlights by us kids may still be forbidden, but she's using one to find her way.

I hang back, like I usually do. That's why I hear what Mr. Philo is saying in a low, firm voice to Mr. Mack.

"You and your staff are going to meet with me tonight."

Mr. Mack starts to say something. Mr. Philo holds up a hand to forestall any comment from the camp director. "Not now. As soon as the campers are in their cabins."

For once, Mr. Mack is not smiling. He looks as if he is sucking on a lemon as he walks away after shouldering his canvas bag. The only ones left here are the Philos, Mr. Wilbur, and myself.

"You can douse the fire now," Mrs. Philo says to Mr. Wilbur, who has been using a stick to spread out the last of the glowing coals in the fire pit. There's a long hiss as he pours the bucket of water and then it is totally dark and silent.

A loud scream echoes through the night.

13

Point

D o I have to tell you that it was Heidi who screamed? *Histrionic* is how Mr. Wilbur referred to her. I didn't have to look that word up to know it means "theatrical."

Theatrical or not, it resulted in a general panic that was finally quelled by the arrival of Mr. Wilbur and the Philos, with me as their light bearer. There'd been no objections to my turning on my big light to lead them around the bend to the mass of confused campers who were not being calmed down by Mrs. Smiler, who had somehow dropped and broken her flashlight in the ensuing confusion. She and the three parent chaperones, all of whom lacked flashlights of their own, were as much in the dark as the kids.

"Settle," Mr. Wilbur says. His familiar, commanding voice has its effect. It gets everyone's attention. Everyone stops trying to talk at once, even Heidi. Admittedly, it helps that Tara has her arm around Heidi's shoulders and her hand over her friend's mouth.

Adrenaline is an amazing thing. When you get frightened or suddenly excited about something, your body pumps it into your blood and you are capable of energetic action. I'm thinking of that as I watch the Philos. They weren't just following me with my light as I ran along the path, they were practically carrying me, leaving Mr. Wilbur behind. I guess a lifetime of taking care of kids means that when they think kids are in trouble they spring into action—and any arthritis or heart problem just has to take a backseat. The two of them are moving among the kids, comforting some, gently teasing others, asking one or two to help them sort things out. I don't know beans about running a camp, but I can tell they are really good at this.

Mr. Wilbur is holding my big flashlight now, its beam making a big circle on the ground in front of him like a heatless campfire. I handed my light to him before I pulled out the Maglite on its Velcro strap that is now fastened around my forehead. Of course it's off right now because I'd be blinding people with it whenever I turned my head in someone's direction. I want to be able to look around now and see who's here without attracting attention to myself. What I have seen so far is worrisome. Two people are not here.

"Everyone calm now?" Mr. Wilbur asks. He holds up his right hand, palm facing forward and puts the index finger of his left hand to his lips. We all know this sign is for us to be quiet and pay attention because he uses it at least three times a day in class. We follow suit with thirty-four eighth-grade hands. Thirty-four index fingers are pressed to silenced lips.

Mr. Wilbur looks over at Mrs. Smiler and the three chaperones who have been counting heads.

"They're all here," Mrs. Smiler says. "No students are missing."

She's being redundant, I think. Saying the same thing twice in two different ways. So am I, for that matter. She's trying to look calm, but she is as nervous as I am.

This, by the way, is one of the things that sucks about being thirteen. You are just old enough to realize that those adults you used to think had all the answers are sometimes just as confused and clueless as you are.

"All right," Mr. Wilbur says. "Good. Now,

Heidi, can you, my dear young lass, tell me why you just screamed like the proverbial Irish banshee?"

That joking tone of his and the thick Irish accent he puts on are just what's needed right now, even though things are serious. It makes even Heidi smile.

"It just scared me when the light went out all of a sudden and then someone grabbed my shoulder from behind and growled at me."

"Who did th—?" Mr. Wilbur starts to say, then shakes his head. "Do I even have to ask?" he says, turning his gaze on Willy Donner.

"Guilty as charged, Mr. W.," Willie says, a little smirk on his face vanishing when Heidi turns and punches him in the left biceps. "Ow, that hurt!"

"People!" Everyone turns back to Mr. Wilbur again. "Let us not go medieval on one other. I'll let that punch go, Heidi. We'll call it justified retribution. Very Old Testament. But here is a new commandment. There shalt be no more hitting, grabbing, or intentional freaking out of thy neighbor. And we are heading back to the main building."

He pauses to scan the crowd. I know he's looking for me and I stand up. His eyes meet mine and he presses his lips together and nods. Even though I am more scared than I have ever been in my entire life, even though I have this feeling of absolute certainty that the worst is still to come, I haven't panicked. Mr. Wilbur can see that. And even though I am the littlest kid in our class, I can see that he is relying on me. I've earned his respect by not acting scared.

It's only logical, though. Like my uncle Jules said to me once, just being scared ought to be enough for anyone. Acting scared on top of it is just a waste of time and energy.

"Drag," Mr. Wilbur says with a smile, tapping himself on the chest. "Baron, you're point man." He knows all about my family's military history and knows I'll understand what he's saying. I'm to go at the head of our column. He'll be the last person, making sure that no one straggles or gets left behind.

"Yessir," I reply, snapping a salute. Then I turn on my forehead Maglite.

With the Philos close behind me, and the other five adults placed at regular intervals in the group, I start leading our group back up the trail past the lightless pole toward the darkened buildings of Camp Chuckamuck.

14

Coleman Lanterns

We're back inside the main building. I'm sitting in the corner near the big fireplace, where a pile of logs burns so hot that I'm sweating. But I'm not about to stop putting logs on the fire. Poe-boy has his head on my knee and I am petting him with one hand and writing with the other. A lot of people seem to have finally fallen asleep. But not me. I couldn't sleep even if I hadn't volunteered to be the fire keeper and be in charge of the Coleman lanterns.

So much has happened since we got back from the fire circle that I don't know where to start. So I'll just make a list in my journal of, as Mr. Wilbur puts it, the pertinent points.

Point #1: Mr. Mack and the one who calls himself Walker White Bear have vanished. So have the other two people I haven't really mentioned before, two men whose names I never got who were brought in by Mr. Mack as counselors. They hung back when our bus came in and none of us, Mr. Wilbur included, ever got a good look at them. We were supposed to be introduced to them. But then everything got crazy. I wonder if they are as incompetent at being camp personnel as the other two. I wonder what they really were hired to do. I wonder what all four of them are doing now.

Point #2: The power lines to the camp seem to have been cut. There's no electricity at all and there's a deep darkness all around because the sky is still clouded over.

Point #3: There is also no emergency power here. A backup generator was supposed to kick in if there was any kind of power failure, like a tree being blown down in a storm over the lines. But as we walked back to the main hall, everything was still dark except for one faint light that appeared to be bobbing on the porch of the building. It turned out to be Mrs. Osgood holding up an old kerosene lamp she'd just lit. The emergency generator was not working, she told us (but not in those few words). When Mr. Philo took a look at it, the first thing he noticed was that the cap was off the gas tank. He put a stick in to measure how much gas was there, and when that stick scraped on something gritty he shook his head in disgust. "It's been sabotaged," he said. "Someone poured sand into the tank."

Point #4: It has been decided that everyone is going to spend the night together here in the main building. Mrs. Osgood brought out half a dozen Coleman lanterns and lit them. Although I have to pump them up every now and then to keep the fuel flowing, and they give off a faint roaring sound, they also provide almost as much light as a 100-watt bulb. So even though the room is filled with strange shadows, it is light enough to give most folks a sense of security. Mr. Wilbur organized details to go to the cabins and bring the foam mattresses from the bunks and all of our stuff into here. The room has been divided into a boys' side and a girls' side, with most of the adults sleeping in a line down the middle of the room where they have set up half a dozen cots. Mr. and Mrs. Philo are in two cots near where I'm sitting in the corner by the fire, furthest away from any of the doors. Mrs. Osgood is on another cot next to the door that leads into the kitchen. It's good that this big building doubles as the dining hall and that the food is also stored in here.

"I have all of my necessities," Mrs. Osgood said, when she met us with her lantern, pointing at a long bag she'd propped in a chair on the porch. "So I calculate that we all can be as snug as a nest of bugs in a rug, what with food and fire. . ." And so on.

And I suppose we are snug in here, even though it is stuffy with all of the windows in the building closed and latched as tight as the doors. No one is supposed to leave the building until dawn. There are two bathrooms in this main building and buckets of water have been brought from the lake so that the cabin toilets can keep functioning.

I guess those are all the main points that I need to list. Everyone is keeping calm. Things are organized to keep everyone safe. But I don't think we are safe. None of the adults are talking about the how and why of all this. Maybe they don't want to alarm us or they think that kids just live in the moment and are not concerned with things like the future. I am, though.

My mind is running through scenarios as I try to put this puzzle together, even though I think there are still pieces missing. There has to be a plan behind this, a logical reason for what has happened so far. I haven't quite figured out what, but I think I know why from eavesdropping on Mr. Wilbur's earlier conversation with Mrs. Smiler. I think the result is supposed to be the end of Camp Chuckamuck and the selling of the property for all that money. That seems obvious to me. Make the camp fail and then it has to be sold.

But there's an even darker side—Mr. and Mrs. Philo. Someone must have tricked those kind old people into coming here and getting trapped. It may mean that the plan behind it all is really an evil one. It may mean that someone wants to do away with them so that they'll no longer be around to prevent their land from being sold. But how do the people who are doing this expect to get away with it?

I think about Mr. Osgood. Even though I just met him and his wife, I know in my heart that they could not be part of a plan to do harm to anyone. He's our biggest hope for rescue because until he reaches the outside no one will know that we're all in trouble and caught here. I look at my watch: 11:00 P.M. He should have reached a phone long ago. People might be on their way here already. Unless he never reached a phone. Unless something happened to him.

I try not to think about that, but turning my thoughts from him turns them back to us. It's like looking away from the edge of a precipice to see a monster creeping up on you. What about the rest of us? Is something supposed to happen to us, too? Will the ones who have planned this see us as witnesses and thus dangerous to them?

I shiver again at where this train of thought is leading me. The only silent witnesses are dead witnesses. Could this be so coldhearted and evil a plan that killing about forty people is part of it? But it couldn't be. That kind of plan wouldn't just be coldhearted. It would be insane.

Suddenly we hear the thud of footsteps on the porch and pounding on the door.

"Let me in!" a voice screams from outside. "He's gone crazy. He's trying to kill me!"

15

Let Me In!

Mrs. Osgood was at that door only a heartbeat after the first anguished scream. She was, quite literally, loaded for bear. It turned out that Mr. Osgood's Betsy was not the only firearm in Camp Chuckamuck after all. There was a 12-gauge pump-action shotgun in Mrs. Osgood's hands. Apparently it had been one of the "necessities" in that long bag of hers. And as she competently worked the pump to jack a shell into the chamber, she also knew how to use it.

Everyone had been freaked out by the sudden banging on the door and the unnerving scream that accompanied it.

"Quiet down," Mr. Wilbur shouted, raising his hands to get everyone's attention.

The tense silence that followed was quickly broken.

"Who's there?" Mrs. Osgood asked.

"For God's sake, it's me," answered a strained voice strangled by fear.

No one made a move to unlock the door.

"Name yourself," Mrs. Osgood said.

"Winston. Winston Mack. Let me in. Hurry. He might be coming. Oh God!"

The Philos, Mr. Wilbur, and Mrs. Osgood all exchanged a quick glance. Then Mrs. Osgood stepped back, keeping the shotgun leveled at the door, as Mr. Wilbur unlocked and quickly swung it open.

It swung open even faster than Mr. Wilbur had intended because the head counselor had been pressing himself against it and looking back over his shoulder. Mr. Mack came stumbling in and sprawled onto the floor, pointing behind himself as he fell.

"Close the door, close it, close it, lock it," he babbled, clutching an old brown backpack to his chest as if it were a shield to protect him. He no longer looked like the smiling, firmly-in-control person he appeared to be when we first saw him. His face was scratched, his shirt torn, and there was blood on his hands.

That was half an hour ago. Although Mr. Wilbur paused long enough to shine the beam of my

big flashlight outside, he saw no threatening figure pursuing. The solid oak door was shut and locked again without incident.

It has taken this long, and two cups of coffee, for Mr. Mack to calm down and start saying anything that makes any kind of sense. He's talking now about how it all started to go wrong.

Mr. Mack is sitting in the kitchen with Mr. Wilbur, the Philos, and Mrs. Osgood, who has not relinquished her 12-gauge. The door, which is partially open, is close to where I have my sleeping bag on the floor. As a result I'm able to listen in on what's being said.

It turns out that one of the things I suspected is true. Mr. Mack and his crew had been hired as ringers. Their mission was to make sure that Camp Chuckamuck failed. Not spectacularly, but through little acts of incompetence and sabotage. Then, when the camp closed down, they'd be paid for their dirty work. Mr. Mack knew nothing about running an outdoor camp, but was someone that the Philos' nephews, who were behind the whole scheme, knew they could count on to do this kind of job.

There's a pause for a moment. Then I hear

Mr. Mack draw in a deep breath.

"You know, you weren't supposed to be here," he says. I can't see who he is directing that statement to, but I assume it is the Philos. His next words prove my assumption right.

"When you came driving in and then the explosion went off," Mr. Mack continues, "that was when I realized things were going wrong. But I didn't know how wrong until an hour ago. That was when he showed me this and then told me who he really is."

"I recognize it as George's," Mrs. Osgood's voice cuts in.

I edge a little closer to the door. I think I know what they're talking about now. I peer through the crack between the door and the jamb. Just as I thought, Mr. Mack is holding up that old backpack he'd been clutching to himself. It's the pack that I saw Mr. Osgood shoulder when he set out on his way to get help. My mouth goes dry and I feel a knot in my stomach. Maybe he just dropped it, I'm thinking. Maybe they just found it where he dropped it. But I know it's not that. This is bad. And it is about to get worse.

"This is just the start, that's what he told me," Mr. Mack continues. He is talking faster now, his tone edging again toward hysteria. "Look," he says, "look at what he showed me. I've got it here inside the pack."

"No!" the shout is from Mrs. Osgood. There's the sudden sound of furniture scraping back, chairs falling. "No!" Mrs. Osgood shouts again.

Everyone is looking toward the kitchen now. We've all heard Mrs. Osgood's voice raised in what I recognize as both anger and despair.

I can't stand it. I have to see what's going on. I push the door open and look through. Mr. Mack has been pushed back into his chair by Mr. Wilbur, whose face is very grim and who is now holding Mrs. Osgood's shotgun. What Mrs. Osgood holds in her hands is the reason for her shout. There are tears in her eyes as she looks at her husband's torn and bloody green jacket.

16

A Name

How can things happen so fast and yet also drag on so slowly at the same time? The crazy flurry of activity that started with that frenzied knocking on the door has been followed by what seems like an interminable period of waiting.

But when I look at my watch I see that only an hour has passed since Mr. Mack stumbled in carrying Mr. Osgood's pack. Only an hour. It feels to me as if it were days ago, as if we've all been waiting here not knowing what is going to happen next for an absolute eternity.

I'm amazed at how calm Mrs. Osgood is now. Or maybe I'm not. I know what it is like to be in denial, to absolutely refuse to accept—despite all the evidence to the contrary—that someone you love has just disappeared and will never come back.

At first, all of the adults in the kitchen had

been so stunned at the sight of Mr. Osgood's jacket that they hadn't thought about the kids in the main room. Everyone had been wakened—and freaked out—by the noise of Mr. Mack's arrival. The confusion hadn't been helped by the sight of him being hustled into the kitchen to be questioned.

Mrs. Smiler and the parent chaperones had just started to get the kids semi-settled down again when Mrs. Osgood's loud "No! No!" had come ringing out of the kitchen. That had stirred things up again and started what sounded like a stampede behind me in the main hall. I didn't even think about what I was doing. I quickly pulled the kitchen door shut, cutting off the sight of Mrs. Osgood and that frighteningly bloody green jacket. A big head bumped against my hip. It was Poe-boy. Together, the big black dog and I turned to face the crowd that actually stopped surging forward and got quiet when I thrust my hand up toward them, palm out.

Asa was at the front of the crowd and he took a hesitant step toward me.

"What's going on?" he said in a shaky voice.

His face was pale. Even though he was still physically taller than me, I realized at that moment both how scared he was and how calm I felt. I also came to the recognition that there really was nothing that scary about him after all. He and his friends, who were huddling together behind him like chickens expecting to get picked off by a hawk, looked like nothing more than frightened little boys. I scanned the other faces in front of me, boys and girls who were my classmates but seemed to be seeing me in a new way. Harle, Cody, Willy, Heidi, Tara, and everyone else. They were all waiting, even Mrs. Smiler and the parent chaperones who were at the back. They wanted reassurance from me, even those boys who'd made me so miserable for so long.

I knew in my heart that if I survived this night I would never be afraid of Asa and his crew again. For the first time I understand something that my mom had told me one day when I came home after being picked on by bigger kids. "Bullies," she said, "act that way because they're afraid."

I also knew, for whatever reason, that what I had to do now was say something to help everyone calm down. "It's okay," I said. "Mr. Mack got hurt, but it wasn't bad. Mr. Wilbur will be out in a second to explain things. Settle, okay?"

It wasn't what you'd call oratorial eloquence. But it worked. The kids calmed down, no longer milling about like a herd of cattle about to head for the nearest cliff, and Mrs. Smiler moved to the front. She raised her hands in a shooing gesture.

"Okay, campers," she said, "you heard the man. Party's over. Everybody retreat to their own crash pad."

Then she turned, smiled at me, and leaned close. "Baron," she said in a soft voice, "you are one cool dude."

A hand grasped my shoulder from behind. "I'll second that," Mr. Wilbur said. "Think I need to say anything to the kids now, Ginny?"

Mrs. Smiler shook her head. "I think it's all groovy for now. What they need to do is get some sleep or they'll be basket cases tomorrow."

"More than they already are?" Mr. Wilbur smiled, but I could tell that his smile was forced.

"What is up?" Mrs. Smiler said.

"We're still figuring it all out." Mr. Wilbur shook his head, his brief smile vanished now. "Let's just say I was a little too right in my misgivings about our new camp director and his staff."

• • •

Misgivings. Not a bad word for how I'm feeling now. Not fear, but a vague uncertainty about what exactly is going to happen next. Aside from being certain that, whatever it is, it is not going to be good.

I've slipped back into the kitchen after the other kids were settled into their sleeping (or lying awake with their eyes wide open while being filled with dread) areas.

Poe-boy, of course, has followed me, although he leaves my side to trot over to Mrs. Osgood, who kneels down and puts her arms around him. Her eyes are moist, but her face looks calm now.

I'm trying to be unobtrusive, but Mr. Wilbur notices me. For a moment I think he's going to ask me to leave the room. Then he shakes his head and smiles in resignation. "You might as well stay and hear the rest of this, Baron," Mr. Wilbur says.

He looks over toward Mr. Mack, slumped in a chair under the alert gaze of Mr. Philo, who is now holding the shotgun. "It won't hurt to have one more pair of eyes keeping watch on our deceptive friend over there."

He motions for me to move over near the door that leads outside. It's on the other side of the room from Mr. Mack, but plenty close to hear all that will be said as he takes a deep, shuddering breath and starts to speak.

"I needed someone who knew the area. That is why I hired him." Mr. Mack doesn't look up. He keeps his gaze on his bloody hands. It is as if he's talking to himself, unaware that anyone else is here. "How could I have known who he was and what he was really up to? It is certainly not my fault, not my fault at all."

"Where's my husband?" a sharp voice cuts in.

Mr. Mack lifts his head in surprise, as if realizing for the first time he's not alone.

"George," Mrs. Osgood reminds him, holding up her husband's coat with her left hand, her right hand on Poe-boy's head. "Where is he now?" The big dog catches the tone in her voice. A growl starts deep in its chest.

Mr. Mack cowers in his chair. "Keep that dog away from me. I don't know. All I know is that Walker handed me that pack with that jacket in it. All he was supposed to do was stop him from calling for help. He wasn't supposed to do anything to him. I didn't know the man was a killer."

"But you never saw my husband's body, did you?" Mrs. Osgood is standing. For some reason she looks less distressed than before as she holds back Poe-boy. The huge black Labrador's growling has gotten much louder now and he is baring his teeth at the man who is shrinking even further back.

"No, no. No, I didn't see his body."

Mrs. Osgood nods. "Good," she says, pulling Poe-boy back with her as she sits down. She smiles over at me. "George is not an easy man to kill, son," she says.

Mr. Philo kicks the leg of Mr. Mack's chair. "You said he was a killer and that you didn't know who he was. I assume you meant that man who calls himself Walker White Bear. Explain what you meant."

Mr. Mack runs a hand through his hair. An officious tone comes back into his voice. "You fail to understand, sir," he says. "Staffing decisions are difficult, even under the best of circumstances. I wasn't able to obtain a résumé, you know. I would not expect a former basketball player to appreciate the difficulty of being an efficient administrator when lacking the requisite access to properly background-check one's employees."

Mr. Wilbur rolls his eyes toward the ceiling. I know what he means by that. This guy, Mr. Mack, is whack.

Mr. Philo nudges the barrel of the shotgun against Mr. Mack's shoulder. "Speak English, pal," he says. "I'm only a dumb ex-jock."

"Careful with that shotgun," Mrs. Osgood warns. "It has a hair trigger. It would smart some if he was to get hit with the load I've got in those shells."

Mr. Philo steps back. "Speak," he says again. "How do you know the man's a killer and who he is?"

"How do I know?" Mr. Mack's face is defiant now, his tone superior. "Do you recall my two other counselors? As soon as they saw that . . ."—he looks toward Mrs. Osgood and her husband's jacket, which is now neatly folded and placed on the floor by her feet—"that blood, I could see from the looks on their faces that they just wanted to get as far away from all of this as they could. They were petty criminals, but they are not murderers. And then when he told us who he really was, that was the last straw for them. They turned and ran." Mr. Mack shudders and puts a hand to his forehead. "He grinned at me when they ran. Then he pulled out that long knife of his and went after them."

Mr. Mack is talking louder and faster now, his hands tapping his knees as he speaks. "Even though they split up, they didn't get far. Either of them. He caught them. Rounded them up. He can see in the dark like some animal. And he's so fast, so strong. I heard their screams. They screamed and they kept screaming. I didn't look back, though. I was running too. Running and running and running until I got back here."

Mr. Mack's voice slows down and then stops like a toy whose battery has run down.

It is more awful than I thought. Everyone is shocked.

But Mr. Philo is not too shocked to speak. "You still didn't answer my second question, pal. Who is he?"

Mr. Mack whispers the name, but everyone hears it. Mrs. Philo raises both hands to her mouth. It's a name we all know.

"Jason Jones."

17

Not a Myth

Jason Jones is real. He's not a myth at all. Mr. Philo is shaking his head. "Of course," he says. "I should have recognized him. But his hair was blond and crew cut when he was a boy and his eyes were blue. Why is he pretending to be an Indian?"

Mrs. Philo pats her husband on the arm. "Hair dye," she says. "Contact lenses. That poor boy always did go in for drama. Remember how he kept changing his name and saying he was really adopted? Can you blame him for that after how he was treated by . . . them? He probably does think he's an Indian now. Poor deluded boy."

Mr. Philo shakes his head again. He's holding the shotgun loosely in one hand with its barrel now pointing at the floor. "He's not a poor boy any longer, Dora," he says. "Even when he was fourteen he was dangerous. How did the state ever let him out? You know he blames us for what happened to him."

"I know," Mrs. Philo says, taking her husband's hand as he leans the shotgun in the corner. "I know, Wally."

What happened to the real Jason Jones, the one who is calling himself Walker White Bear? Mr. Wilbur doesn't know the real story any more than I do, and we both listen as the Philos fill us in about the "poor boy" who was the son of a camp cook and caretaker here at Chuckamuck over twenty years ago. That cook and the caretaker were new and they showed up with their gangly teenage son in tow, a big boy who was withdrawn and wouldn't make eye contact. The Philos, who had always been kind-hearted, decided to let Jason take part in all the activities as if he were one of the regular campers.

"We thought it would do the lad good," Mr. Philo says. "I come from humble beginnings myself."

But they'd missed two things. The first was how badly he had been abused by someone, really badly abused. They first began to realize that when they noticed the scars on his arms and legs the day Jason came for swimming lessons. Scars from burns.

"An accident," Jason's father said when Mr. Philo asked him about it. "The kid's always been clumsy." From that day on, no matter how hot it was, Jason wore long-sleeved shirts and slacks and didn't come to any more swimming classes.

The second thing the Philos failed to notice was that the big, shy boy's personality was what people now call bipolar, with a good amount of paranoid schizophrenia mixed in. The other campers hadn't tortured him or played mean tricks on him at all. He'd imagined all that and come to the Philos time after time to complain about what the other kids were doing to him. But it wasn't true.

What was true was that Jason Jones really was being abused by his own parents, even though he denied it when the Philos asked him directly about it. Then the Philos's cat disappeared. For a day or two they thought a coyote might have gotten it, until Jason said in an innocent voice, "Did anyone look back in the clearing along the trail to the spring?"

Mr. Philo found their cat—what was left of it—in that clearing. The footprints in the soft earth matched those of only one person.

The stories about Jason killing other

campers weren't true. It went no further than that cat. The Philos brought in the sheriff's office and people from Social Services. All three members of the Jones family were interviewed and at one point Jason confessed to killing the Philos's cat—and other small animals—over the past years. He also admitted that it was his father who beat and tortured him whenever he got drunk—which was every weekend. It was all put on tape, which was good since Jason later denied all of it and claimed that the Philos were the ones who had mistreated him. They were out to get him and his family, he said. It was all their fault.

The Joneses were fired from Camp Chuckamuck. Jason was put on medication and sent into foster care, even though he begged to stay with his mother and father.

"We kept up with what happened to them through the papers," Mrs. Philo sighs. "It was such a tragedy."

Jason Jones was finally allowed to go back to his family. He was nineteen years old by then, a huge, hulking man and no longer a little boy. Somehow, despite his medical history, he'd been accepted in the Army and had been to boot camp and trained for the Rangers. Then he was home on a weekend leave.

"Jason's story," Mr. Philo says, "was that intruders broke in and did . . . what was done. But the story didn't hold up. He was tried for the murder of his parents and because of the way the trial went, because of the unbalanced way he acted and the outrageous things he said . . ."

"Why, at one point he stated that Wally and I were the ones who'd gone there and done that dreadful deed," Mrs. Philo interjects.

Mr. Philo nods. "In the end a decision was made to send him to a secure medical facility instead of a regular prison."

"We thought he'd spend his life in there," Mrs. Philo adds.

"But apparently not," Mr. Philo concludes.

A long silence follows. I think I know the question that is in everyone's mind. But no one speaks up, so I do.

"Well, what do we do now?" I ask, stepping up to the table. I'm surprised at how calm and clear my voice is.

Mr. Wilbur actually chuckles. "Baron," he said, "thanks for cutting through the gloom. You have hit the nail on the proverbial head. Any ideas?"

A chair scrapes on the floor and I turn to look. Mrs. Osgood has just stood up and walked over to one of the cupboards. "I've got one," she says, as she rummages around and pulls out a cell phone. "We can call for help. The Sheriff's Department can have a mountain rescue helicopter in here by first light."

"Cell phones don't work around here," Mr. Wilbur says.

"They don't work most places, young fella," Mrs. Osgood replies, a no-nonsense tone in her voice. "But George found one place where you can pick up a signal. He calls it the Bear Seat. Look."

Everyone gathers around the table as Mrs. Osgood pulls out a map of the trails and unfolds it. "Up here," she says, "just a random scoot. Not more than a mile and a half."

"I remember that spot," Mr. Philo says. "It's the west lookout on the side of Pisgah Mountain. There is a rock slab there that looks rather like a bench."

"Ayup," Mrs. Osgood says. "The bears like to come at sunset and sit there. That is why George calls it the Bear Seat."

Mr. Philo taps the map with a long index finger. "I know that place also. I always led our trail hikes past there, though I never saw a bear."

"You never was an Abenaki, either," Mrs. Osgood says. Her voice is light and teasing, which is strange seeing as how her husband's bloody jacket is still resting on the floor behind her. Or perhaps not so strange because she is so certain he's alive. Then again, everything is weird right now—this night, the way we are talking. My head is swimming from the strangeness of it all.

Mr. Philo smiles back at her. "Point taken. All I am saying is that it is an easy hike to get there. It's only a hundred yards off the main marked trail. I could do it in the dark."

Mrs. Philo is patting her husband's arm. He turns to look at her.

"What?" he says.

"Not with those knees and"—she pats his chest—"this heart, dear."

"All right. Point taken." He looks at Mr. Wilbur. "So Kirk will be the one to do it. Think you can locate that spot?"

"Piece of cake," Mr. Wilbur says. "Even a child could find the way."

He turns to Mr. Mack, who is still slouched in his seat at the other end of the room, a blank, uncaring look on his face. "Does he have any weapons? Did any of you bring any firearms?"

Mr. Mack looks up like a man waking from an unpleasant dream. Slowly, he shakes his head. "No, no. None of us had guns. We never planned violence. All he has is that big knife of his." Mr. Mack's whole body shivers. "He said the only way to kill is hand to hand. Guns are for cowards."

"Good that we have the only gun, then," Mr. Philo says.

"For all the good it will do you," Mrs. Osgood adds.

I suppose she's right. Whoever takes that phone will have to avoid getting ambushed by Walker White Bear or Jason Jones or whoever that homicidal maniac thinks he is. Even a shotgun may not be enough protection.

Mr. Wilbur takes the phone from her. "Maybe we could do something out front to draw attention there. Then I can slip out the back, circle past the lake and hit the trail over there." He lifts up the big flashlight, then puts it down. "Baron, I should probably borrow that little head lamp of yours. A small light like that is less likely to be seen. I can just flick it on now and then to find the silver trail markers."

I'd forgotten I was still wearing the flashlight. I take it off my forehead and hand it to him. I wish there was something more I could do or even say to help.

Mr. Wilbur turns back and reaches toward the corner. A perplexed look comes over his face. "Where is it?"

"Are you looking for this?" a sarcastic voice says.

We all turn to see Mr. Mack, his back straight, not slouching in terror and despair any longer. There is a very unpleasant smile on his face. The shotgun he's holding is pointed at all of us.

18

An Act

We all stare at the man who is so unlike the cringing figure we'd seen just moments before. It was all an act. He's fooled us again.

Mrs. Osgood takes a step toward him and he points the shotgun at her chest.

"I wouldn't do that if I were you," he says. He's talking like a clichéd villain in a bad movie, but he's no less dangerous for that.

Mr. Wilbur reaches out to take Mrs. Osgood's arm and pull her back so that she is standing next to me.

Mr. Mack smiles. It's not the sunny, insincere smile he showed everyone earlier in the day when he was playing the part of the genial camp director. This grin is that of a wolf that has just trapped its prey. He motions with the shotgun at the table.

"Sit, all of you."

Mrs. Osgood reaches behind my back as she moves toward the table, pushing something hard under my belt. I slip my hand back there to feel it and know what it is right away. No one else has noticed this exchange between us. Mr. Mack doesn't pay attention to the fact that when I sit down it is not at the table but on the stool in the corner that is closest to the back door. I'm by a window where I can look outside into the dark night. I'm just a little kid. No threat at all.

Everyone except Mr. Mack is sitting now. I wonder how he expects to control this situation all by himself. What if one of the parents or Mrs. Smiler comes in? What about all the kids out there?

Someone taps twice lightly on the back door.

"Now who could that be?" Mr. Mack says, his smile getting even broader. Without lowering the shotgun, he backs up to the door. He taps on it three times, unlatches it, and then steps back again, never taking his eyes off the four adults sitting at the table.

The door opens, but the skinny man with thinning blond hair who steps through is not the one I've been dreading to see. It's one of

Mr. Mack's supposedly slaughtered assistants. The sleeves of his khaki shirt are rolled up now and I can see the tattoo of a cartoon canary with an arrow through its heart on his right bicep.

"Back from the grave so soon, Cal?" Mr. Mack smiles.

"Hunh?" the man says. "What do you mean?"

"A private jest," Mr. Mack says. "Where's your equally undeceased sibling?"

"What?" Cal says. I can see now why he and Mr. Mack's other assistant hung back without saying anything earlier in the day. Plainly Cal was not hired for his mental acuity. As Grama Kateri might put it, he's a few potatoes short of a bushel.

"Where . . . is . . . your . . . brother . . . Marlon?" Mr. Mack asks, his voice insultingly slow as if talking to a three-year-old. Cal doesn't catch it.

"Oh," he says, pointing. "Out there."

"Bring . . . him . . . in," Mr. Mack says.

"Oh, okay." Cal goes back outside as Mr. Mack shakes his head.

"Monosyllables work best when communicating with morons," he says, looking at the

Philos and Mr. Wilbur as if asking for their sympathy. "It is so hard to get good help these days." He pauses, waiting for a response.

No one says anything, but Mrs. Osgood, who is being ignored right now by Mr. Mack, makes a shooing gesture toward me with her hand under the table. I understand what she means.

"Well," Mr. Mack says, his tone that of someone who loves to hear himself speak, "if no one is going to ask, I should just tell you. That tale about my murderous associate, who remains lurking somewhere out there in the woods, terminating his coworkers, was a bit of a fable. As you can see, Cal and Marlon remain alive and well. I also prevaricated just a bit about our being unarmed. Marlon is in possession of a pistol and is, no doubt because he lacks the intellect to understand the concept of consequences, unafraid to use it. That turned out to be, quite frankly, fortuitous. I must confess that we did have a major labor dispute with our ersatz aboriginal colleague. Different goals, you see. Lucre on our parts, slaughter on his."

As convoluted as Mr. Mack's diction is, I think I understand what he's saying. Mr. Mack and his two men are doing this to make money. They really did have a falling-out with Jason Jones or Walker White Bear or whoever he thinks he is, because his aims are darker and bloodier. He wants to kill us all while the others are just in it for profit. From the looks on the faces of Mr. Wilbur and the Philos, they grasp the situation too.

Mr. Wilbur finally says something, and even though it also sounds like it's from a bad movie script, it is appropriate.

"How do you expect to get away with this?"

"Extremely well paid," Mr. Mack replies. "The Bahamas are quite pleasant at this time of the year, you know. There will be a substantial deposit in my bank account in the Cayman Islands. And as for Cal and Marlon, a return to incarceration, alas, seems fated to be their eventual recompense. There will be many witnesses left to tell at least part of the story."

Many witnesses, I think. But not everyone. Even though Mr. Mack drew the line at mass murder, death is part of his scenario too. The Philos have to die so their land will be inherited by the nephews who are behind this whole plot. Mr. Wilbur and Mrs. Osgood and I have all heard too much. He's telling us all of this because he is planning on wiping out everyone in this room. I'm even more certain now of what I have to do, do or die trying. An act of desperation.

I shift my weight onto my feet and lean just a little toward the door. I'm quietly taking deep breaths, getting ready. I turn my eyes away from the light of the hissing Coleman lanterns, and focus on the darkness outside the window. Two flashlights make bobbing circles on the ground that come closer and closer toward the building, and pass the window.

Two light raps come again on the back door.

Mr. Mack sighs. "It is already unlocked, Cal," he says in disgust. "Just come in."

The door opens and Cal enters, followed closely by his brother, Marlon, who, though a little brawnier and darker-haired, is a close copy of his twin brother. His sleeves are rolled up too. His tattoo shows a cartoon mouse with a dagger stuck through its head. It's funny the kind of details that your mind takes in, the way things seem to move in slow motion, when you do something dangerous or foolish.

Like what I'm doing right now. I'm off my stool, ducking under the arms of Cal and Marlon as they grab at me and miss. Marlon swings the pearl-handled pistol in his left hand as if it is a club, trying to hit my head. The barrel grazes my cheekbone, drawing blood, but I'm past him. I sense as much as see Marlon raising his gun and cocking it.

"No," Mr. Mack roars. "Watch them. I'll get the boy."

Not if I can help it. My feet thud down the steps and hit the hard ground. It's dark, but even in the darkest night there's always some light. My eyes have adjusted, more than the eyes of Mr. Mack. I'm counting on that as I see the slight glitter of water in front of me and know that I'm already next to the lake. I'm a fast runner. They won't be able to catch me. Even if they shoot at me, it's hard to hit a moving, dodging small person in the dark. Or so I hope.

The beam of a flashlight sweeps over me. I feel a searing pain stab into my back and shoulders at almost the same time as I hear the thud of the shotgun blast. I take a few staggering steps on the wood planks of the dock before I fall. The black water closes over my head.

19

Quiet

The cold water revives me as soon as I plunge into it. Somehow I'm not dead. Even though my back and shoulders smart, it doesn't hurt that much now. Maybe I'm just in shock and can't feel the pain. But my mind is working just fine and it tells me to dive deeper, to turn back toward the dock and swim underwater. I've always been a great swimmer and I can stay underwater for a long time. My hands feel the pilings of the dock and I pull myself under it. Then, slowly, I allow myself to float toward the surface, just enough so that my head is above water and I can take a breath again. I force myself not to gasp as I look up.

Through the narrow cracks between the boards I can see a flashlight's beam directed over the dock and out onto the water. Then comes the *thump-thump-thump* of heavy feet. I take a deep breath and pull myself underwater again. I don't want to take a chance on being seen through the cracks between the boards. I start to count slowly. One and one thousand. Two and one thousand. Looking up, I can see a faint gleam of light and I know that Mr. Mack is using my big flashlight to look under the dock.

Forty and one thousand. Forty-one and one thousand. The water above my head becomes dark again. But I wait and keep counting.

Ninety and one thousand, ninety-one and one thousand. I rise to the surface again and listen. I can hear a voice, far off now.

"Did you get him?" it calls.

"Blew him into the water." Mr. Mack's self-satisfied voice comes from right above me. He's still standing on the dock, shining the light out onto the surface of the lake. "I don't see his body, but not to fret. From that range he'll have a hole in him the size of Montana."

Mr. Mack chuckles and then steps back off the dock. I hear the sound of his feet growing fainter and then the back door of the building being shut.

I don't climb up on the dock. No sense in taking chances by exposing myself. I wade a little farther past the boats, crawl out onto the little beach behind them, and rest on my hands and knees. My back smarts too much for me to lie down on it. But that's all. It just burns a little. I unbutton my shirt and peel it off my shoulders. It sticks like sunburned skin being pulled off. But when I feel the shirt with my hands there's no big hole in it like you'd expect from a full load of shotgun pellets. Just lots and lots of little tiny holes.

Rock salt! I almost laugh out loud. That was what Mrs. Osgood meant when she said that it would smart if she shot Mr. Mack. When you just want to use a shotgun to scare away bears without really injuring them, you take out the iron pellets and then refill the shell with a load of rock salt. That was what I had been shot with. I'm okay!

But I am now shivering like crazy and my teeth are chattering. My body had been chilled by the lake and the night air is starting to feel colder. My wet clothes are not helping. I'm going to go into hypothermia unless I keep moving.

I reach one shaking hand to my back pants pocket where I stowed the cell phone before I made my mad dash. It's one of the many pockets in my baggy cotton pants that has a zipper on it. When I pull the phone out it only seems a little damp. It should work just fine. I reach into another pants pocket and my fingers find the little carved bear. Feeling it makes me calmer, even though I'm still cold. I leave it there, and trying a third pocket, I find one of my disposable flashlights. I bend to shield it with my body, cup my hand over the end, and press the switch. The light glows red through the skin of my hands. It's working. I turn it off, stand up and begin to feel my way along the shore toward the Osgoods' cabin.

Moving helps some, but I am still quivering from the cold when I reach the edge of the building. I make my way around to the back and flick my light on for just a second. I almost say *Hallelujah!* out loud at what I see. Just as I'd hoped, those old clothes that belonged to the Osgoods' son are still hanging there.

I'm shaking so much that I don't even try to unbutton my shirt. I just rip it and my T-shirt off, à la Hulk Hogan in one of his wrestling matches, and drop them on the ground. I yank the closest shirt off the line and put it on. There's no pants, so I'll just have to make do with my wet ones. But I use a third shirt like a towel as I sit down and pull off my sneakers, strip off my socks, replace them with a wool pair from the line, and put my sneakers back on. Then I take a second shirt and put it on over the first.

The second shirt comes almost down to my knees and that's good. My fingers are no longer numb and I button it up all the way. By the time I'm done I'm no longer shaking.

I flick on the light again and direct it toward the trail edge, where it reflects off a silver trail marker. I quickly turn it off. I'm not so worried now about the three men in the kitchen of the main camp building. The Osgoods' cabin is still between them and me. They won't see this light. But there is someone else to fear in the darkness.

I know in the logical part of my mind that Walker White Bear or Jason Jones is not a creature out of some old story. He's not some terrible being who can turn himself from a human into a bear. He's just—ha, just—a crazy person who wants to kill every human being here at Camp Chuckamuck. Now that makes me feel a lot better, doesn't it? Except I am worrying in another part of my mind that he is that and more.

I worry that he can see in the dark and that he is out there stalking me right now. I worry that his senses are more than those of an ordinary human. I'm bleeding, from my cheek and from the dozens of little puncture wounds on my back. And the smell of blood, the scent of a wounded animal, always attracts a predator.

Keep moving, I tell myself. Just keep your ears open.

Listen. My dad and mom, Uncle Jules, and Grama Kateri have said that to me so many times. In the old days, being a good listener could mean the difference between life and death. I've always remembered that, but it has never meant as much to me as it does now. I'm moving as quickly as I can without making a lot of noise. I'm thinking about what Uncle Jules and Dad both taught me about how to move quickly on a trail in the woods. Stay low, roll your feet, don't bring them down hard. Keep your hands up and slightly ahead of you.

It's no longer completely dark now. The first light of dawn is starting to show above the trees. I can see without flicking the flashlight on every ten or twenty steps. I try to keep my vision wide like Dad told me he did when he was in enemy territory. Use peripheral vision so that I see things off to the sides rather than just straight ahead like I'm looking down a tunnel.

Turn my body every now and then to see what is behind me. Keep going. Keep listening. Stay aware.

Birds are beginning to stir in the trees, making their first tentative sounds before bursting into sunrise song. I no longer hear so many noises from the woodland creatures that come out at night, scurrying in the leaves and brush. People who've never been in the forest think it is quiet at night, but many animals feed and move about more at night than during the day. I've already spooked a little group of deer into bounding off through the woods, almost blundered into a porcupine that made a little moaning sound, rattling his quills against the brush as he moved away. In a way, the sounds and presence of those animals has been reassuring to me. It only becomes totally silent when a hunter's presence makes itself felt.

It's getting quiet now, though. The forest around me feels something and I feel it too. The trail, although it is rutted deeply by countless feet following it over the years, is steeper now. I'm having to use my hands as I climb up rocks and around the roots of trees that splay out over the bedrock stones like huge fingers. It's hard to turn around and listen when I'm climbing like this. Something is watching me. I haven't seen anything. But I can feel it in my bones. I'm not alone.

I slowly settle myself back on the tree root I was about to scramble over. I move my head, taking in the whole circle around me. Just as I start turning to my left, I freeze. Another set of eyes is focused straight at me. Dark, deep eyes. There, no more than twenty feet away, its presence as sudden as if it just materialized out of thin air, is a huge black bear.

≫ 20 ≪

Battery

I look back at the bear. I know that staring into the eyes of a wild animal isn't a good idea. That animal might take it as a challenge. But I can't seem to make myself look away. Ever since I can remember I've wanted to see a bear in the wild. I know how risky it might be to get this close to a bear, so close it could be on top of me in only a few steps. But compared to the humans not far from here who would gladly kill me, this bear seems positively benevolent. I don't feel threatened.

But, then again, maybe I should. Because of the way that bear is sitting, like a person might sit, leaning back against a big birch tree with her hind legs thrust out in front of her and her front paws held up to her chest, I can see she is a female bear. She's so close I can see not only the dugs on her belly where her little ones would nurse, but also that the thin hair around them seems wet. Maybe I should talk to her in a low, reassuring voice. Tell her I mean no harm. Greet her as a relative because I belong to the Bear Clan.

Something growls near me. Then I feel a tug on the toe of my right boot. I don't move my head, but I look down with my eyes and see what I thought I would. I am in deep doo-doo, I think. There, chewing on the toe of my shoe, is a baby bear. A chirping sound comes from behind me and something nudges my back. I don't have to look this time to know that it's the first little bear's brother or sister. I'd better not look back. Moving right now is the worst thing I can do. I'm in the most dangerous place a human being can be in the wild—directly between a mother bear and her cubs.

These are not tiny bears. After all, they were born last February as hairless, blind little creatures during their mother's hibernation. They've had a whole spring and summer of being fed and protected by their mother, demanding little brats that have run her ragged as they get into everything in sight. Now, in October, they probably weigh about sixty pounds each and they're strong little buggers.

Just as I think that, the bear cub behind me

thrusts both of its front feet hard against my back at the same time as the first cub yanks hard on my boot. I go sprawling down the slope. As I roll, closing my eyes and covering my face with my hands, a thought goes through my mind. *Be careful not to wish too hard for anything, otherwise you just might get it.* I hadn't understood what Grama Kateri meant when she said that to me one day. Now I do. I wanted to see bears, but not like this, where seeing them might be the last thing I'll ever see!

Whomp! My rolling is stopped, but not gently, by the trunk of a hemlock as my back, torn and bruised by the rock salt, hits hard against it. It hurts so much that I have to bite my lip to keep from shouting. My eyes are still closed. If I don't open them, maybe the mother bear won't see me. That is what I'm thinking. Smart, eh? But at least I'm no longer between the mother and her babies so I have to be safer. Right?

Wrong. This game is too interesting for them to quit now. I hear the thumping of their feet just before they land on top of me. They're chuckling, woofing, chirping, almost singing as they maul me, batting at me with their paws, pulling at my shirt and my baggy pants with their teeth. I'm being bruised, but they're not trying to hurt me. They aren't biting hard enough to draw blood, and although their claws are scratching me, it's in fun. I keep pushing them away from my face to keep their sharp little teeth away from my nose and cheeks, which seem particularly attractive to them. I can smell their sweet milk breath, which is almost like that of nursing puppies. I keep my hands open, pushing, not grabbing. I try to sit up against their playful onslaught. They are so comical that even though I am getting bounced around like a rag doll I have to laugh out loud. I can't help it.

Huh-wooof! That sound between a cough and a roar is so loud that it stuns me, but it has the exact opposite effect on the two cubs. They know the sound of a mother bear warning her cubs to seek shelter. The two of them yelp and claw their way up the trunk of the nearest tree. Naturally, it is the hemlock I am propped up against. And once again I am in between them and their mother with one significant difference. Rather than being twenty feet away, the large, very imposing mother bear is now standing right over me. I should have used my tree-climbing skills and scuttled up after them. But it's too late for that now.

Hnnnnrrrhhh. The sound she makes isn't a growl. Even though her paws are on either side of me and I can feel the heat of her body, I'm not afraid anymore.

"My relative," I say to her in Mohawk. "Take pity on me."

Almost in slow motion, she opens her mouth and bites me on the shoulder. Her sharp teeth spear through the cloth of both shirts and into the flesh of my shoulder. It hurts, but I don't cry out. She lifts me up, shakes me once—not as hard as she might—and tosses me off to the side. Away from the tree where her cubs have sought refuge.

But she doesn't do what a bear should do then. She doesn't follow up with a mauling attack. She just stands there, swaying her head from side to side.

Unnh-unnn, unnh-unnn, she says.

I stand up slowly, moving backward as best I can up the slope. Maybe I should repeat that sound, move my head back and forth the way she's doing. It's what Mr. Fadden told me to do when a bear greets you. But if I tried it right now I'd probably fall and roll back down the slope. My legs are shaky and I'm feeling as if I don't know whether to laugh or cry. For some reason there are tears in my eyes. I'm a victim of assault and battery at the paws and claws and teeth of three bears. But I feel on the one hand as if I have been blessed and on the other as if I should turn, go back down the slope, and wander off into the forest with them like the little orphan boy in that old Mohawk story. I keep moving.

The mother bear stays there, watching me as I climb farther up the trail. Her two cubs scoot down from the tree to stand next to her. One of them takes a step as if to go up the trail after me and she quickly cuffs him back behind her.

Finally I come to a place where the way is so steep that I have to grasp at a tree branch and pull myself up. I have to turn my gaze away from them only for a second, but when I turn back to look, the bears are gone. It's so sudden that I wonder for a moment if I've imagined it all. Then I feel the throb in my left shoulder. It is beginning to ache from the puncture wounds made by the mother bear's canine teeth. My clothing is torn, my hands and arms are bleeding from a dozen scratches. Yet, beaten up as I might be, I feel as if I have been given a gift at the start of this strange day. I turn and keep climbing toward the place where the light coming from the east is making the exposed rock slope glow as gold as the sun.

I'm still following the silver trail markers. The Bear Seat isn't far from here. There's a branch in the trail I have to find to get to it. Then a thought comes to me. The phone. Did I lose it when I had my encounter with the bears? I slap my hand against my pocket in a moment of panic. It's still there.

I flick it open and press a key. *Beep!* And a light comes on. Great! A series of musical notes plays as a pattern of circles forms, expanding in waves. Then the digital display appears.

And my heart sinks.

LOW BATTERY, it reads.

21

Still

My heart sinks. I haven't yet reached the
place where the trail turns off to the
Bear Seat. I can't leave this phone
turned on, draining what little charge is left. I
quickly press the off key on the phone. That
series of musical notes accompanies the appear-
ance of the word GOODBYE in the center of
those concentric circles before the screen goes
blank.

This time it crosses my mind that here in
the quiet of the woods the sound of that cell
phone melody is awfully loud. It is so unlike
any natural sound that it would immediately
call attention to itself. And it could be heard
from a long way away. As I'm thinking that, I
hear a noise coming from above me. It's not
another cell phone. It's the thumping sound of
heavy feet on the bedrock of the trail. Someone
or something large is coming down the trail in

my direction. It's coming fast, drawn by the sound of the cell phone.

I can't see yet who or what is making that sound. The narrow hiking trail dips and rises, moving back and forth between the trees and boulders. That means, though, that I haven't been seen yet. I shove the phone back into my pocket and move off the trail as quickly and quietly as I can, keeping low. I see a big dead pine that has fallen and is angled down the slope. I quickly decide to crawl over it and then slide beneath, burying myself in the deep pine needles, twigs, and leaf litter to lay flat. I think I'm hidden from sight. I just hope I haven't made too much noise digging down into the dry debris that gravity and the mountain winds have gathered up against this log.

I realize that there's a very small open space in front of my face, under the fallen trunk. I may be able to look through it and see the part of the trail where I was sitting before. I just have to press myself down a little. Pine needles and broken pieces of pine cone stick into the wound on my cheek that was made by the gun barrel and reopened during my encounter with the bears. My bitten shoulder aches as I flatten even more against the ground.

It's so painful to do this, but it's worth it. Just as I'd hoped, through one eye, I can see the trail through the screen of fallen debris. But what I see almost makes me gasp in dismay. There, crouched on the trail on all fours, looking more like an animal than a human being, is Jason Jones. He sees something on the ground that makes his mouth widen into a grin, showing his sharp teeth. He reaches down with one hand and picks up a yellow beech leaf. I'm close enough to see the yellow of that leaf is blotched with red. Oh, no. The red on that leaf is blood from the cut on my cheek. He holds the leaf up to his mouth and licks it with his tongue.

Then he turns in my direction with a quickness that is so uncanny, so threatening, that I close my eyes. I don't want to see him. But I still hear what he growls in a low voice that is so calm and cold that I shiver involuntarily.

"I've tasted you," he says. "You can't escape me."

I don't move. He hasn't seen me. Stillness is my salvation. He's using his voice the way an owl calls at night, hoping to spook some small hidden prey animal into panicked flight. I'm small, too, buried deep in the leaves and brush under this log. But I won't run like some foolish deer

mouse. I'll keep still. So still.

There's a thump against the log. I open my eye just a crack and see his legs through the screen of brush. He's right next to the log now, leaning over it. I can hear his heavy breathing above me. My heart is thumping so hard in my chest that I'm afraid he'll hear it. But I don't move.

I can't be seen, I think. I can't be seen.

The log rocks as he presses down on it and then moves back. His legs vanish from sight.

"You're not far from here," he says. But I can hear that he's farther away when he says it. "I'm going to get you."

No, you're not, I think.

His voice is moving downslope, down the trail, where there are more drops of blood that mark where I'd been. He's no longer following me. He's backtracking.

He may think he's a bear, but he's not as quiet as one. His feet are breaking twigs and dislodging small stones that rattle down the slopes below. I wait until I can no longer hear his voice or any sounds of his passage.

I slide out from beneath the log and rise up slowly, a finger's width at a time, into a crouch. I'm alone again. I can feel it as much as see it.

He may turn and come back, but I have a little time, maybe enough to get to the Bear Seat.

I make very little noise as I get back onto the trail and start to climb. I'm extra careful not to dislodge any loose rocks that might roll down. It's easier to be quiet now because as I rise in elevation and the trees get smaller there's less brush and the trail is worn down to smooth stone.

I pause when I get to the top of the trail where it widens into an expanse of ledge. I lean against a big boulder. My legs feel shaky and my calves are cramping up. I'm breathing hard and my stomach hurts. I press my hand against it and it makes a growling sound. All of a sudden I realize how hungry I feel. It's been twelve hours since I ate anything and I've expended so much energy.

I can't stop now, though. There're two trail markers on the cedar tree ahead of me. One is silver, the other is red. I remember the conversation around the table before Mr. Mack picked up the shotgun. The red marker indicates the start of the short trail to the Bear Seat.

I look back down the mountain along the way I just came. A blue jay is sitting in a tree fifty yards below me. A red squirrel is digging at the base of a pine farther down. It's reassuring to see them. They wouldn't be so calm if something was approaching from below them. A soft wind blows across my face. The sun that is now a hand's width above the horizon shines through a gap in the clouds. It's beautiful at this moment and I draw in a slow, grateful breath for these few seconds of peace. I wish I could just sit down, lean against this tree, close my eyes, and sleep.

But I can't stop. I have to keep going. I take a few steps onto the trail to the Bear Seat. Suddenly, a figure rises up and looms above me. A bloody hand grasps my arm.

22

Help

I stare up in disbelief at the bloodied face of the man who leans on me as he holds my arm.

"*Seh'kon*, Awasosis," he says. "Hello, Little Bear. What be you doing here?" Then his legs start to buckle. I step forward and put my arm around his waist, helping him to sit back down and lean against the smooth trunk of an old dead cedar. He's lost his hat somewhere. There's just a kerchief around his head. It was red already, but it's a darker red now from the blood that has matted his thick white hair.

Mr. Osgood lifts his hand to gesture at his head. "Scalp wounds do bleed some," he says. "Looks worse than it is." He slaps his leg. "It's the knee that has put a hitch in my git-along. Got tore up when a tree fell on it when I was a sprat. Rolling down that cliff didn't help it none."

Mr. Osgood looks me over as I kneel there beside him. "It appears to me you've had a mite of rough handling yourself, son."

I fill him in as quickly as I can about the events at Camp Chuckamuck and my escape, my encounter with the bears, and how close I came to being caught by you-know-who.

Mr. Osgood chuckles. "And here I thought being cut and falling down the mountain earned me the medal for having the worst day. You have trumped me, lad. I believe you need this more'n I do."

He unbuttons the pocket of his khaki shirt and pulls out a big carob-coated protein bar. "I always carry a few of these when I head out on a hike," he says, as I tear off the wrapper with my teeth and then try to control myself from just wolfing it down and making myself sick. With each bite I can feel my energy returning. It's probably as much from realizing I'm not alone out here as it is from the food.

While I eat, Mr. Osgood gives me a quick rundown of what happened to him. Mr. Mack, Cal, and Marlon had laid an ambush for him on the trail, but he'd gotten wind of it.

"Even those what think themselves country boys," he chuckled, "have a hard time sitting still and keeping quiet in the woods."

He had quietly circled around them and reached the place where Matilda, his four-wheeler was stored. That was when he had two unpleasant surprises. The first was seeing that Matilda's wires had been pulled. The second was when he was rushed by the big man who had been lying in wait behind the shed where Matilda was stored.

"I may not be as young as I was," Mr. Osgood said, "but even an old woodchuck knows how to duck."

The first knife slash had only cut his scalp. He'd been able to bring up his .22 and get off a shot.

"Hit him right in the chest, but he just stopped for a moment. Then he grinned at me, said something about how bullets couldn't kill him, and started walking at me slow." Mr. Osgood shook his head. "Hearing that made me decide to see how a rifle butt would suit him. While he was clearing his head from having Betsy slammed up against the side of his skull, I hightailed it for the high country."

But even though Mr. Osgood knew the woods and trails better than anyone, the one who called himself Walker White Bear had managed to catch up to him where the trail went above a steep drop-off.

"So I shucked my pack and my jacket and took a dive, figuring I'd just slide down the rock face," Mr. Osgood says with a wry shake of his head. "But I figured wrong. Twenty years ago I could have managed fine, but this stiff leg of mine played me false. Caught my heel and started to tumble. Wasn't that hard to lay limp like all my bones was broke when I hit the bottom. It's a ways down into that gulley, so I suppose that is why he just left me for dead."

"I'm glad you're alive," I say. I suppose it's a silly thing to say, but it makes Mr. Osgood smile.

"Why, thank you, son. I guess that means we two are in total agreement. But what are you doing up here?"

I've forgotten to tell him about the phone. "Trying to make it to the Bear Seat." I pull the cell phone out of my pocket, open it, and press the button. This time nothing happens at all. It has gone totally dead. What little hope I'd been feeling dies.

"Don't look so sad, I've got me a backup," Mr. Osgood says, handing me a second cell phone that is an exact twin to the one I'm holding. "It's all set to go," he says. "She'd tan my hide if she heard me say it, but Mrs. Osgood is a mite more forgetful than me when it comes to keeping her cell phone charged."

I take the cell phone and follow Mr. Osgood's direction. There's only one way up to the Bear Seat where he'd been heading at a crawl to make the call I'm now determined to complete. I'm going alone because it's too much of a scramble for him now with his hurt knee. He's staying hidden near the branch in the trail to keep watch.

My feet feel sure and confident as I climb. It's almost as if I'm flying as I go up the trail and scale the steep cliff side that leads to my objective. I'm not even breathing hard when I reach the spot. It's easy to recognize, not just because it's a slab of rock that is flat as a bench and gives the widest view I've yet seen off the side of this mountain. Someone, who knows how long ago, has carved into the stone the rough outline of a sitting bear.

I'm dialing the phone. The call goes through. I'm talking to the 911 operator. It's almost as if I'm in a dream now. I'm not even sure what I'm saying, but I must be making sense because the operator asks me first one question and then another as I answer her. My voice is calm. I think that helps convince her I'm telling the truth. Another voice comes on the line.

"Young man," it says, "this is the sheriff."

I tell him about Mr. Mack and the others holding the students and teachers at gunpoint in the main cabin at Camp Chuckamuck and how I got away and climbed up here on the mountain to make my call for help.

"Son," the sheriff says. "Just sit tight. We're sending help."

I sit there for a moment after closing the phone and putting it into my pocket. A red-tailed hawk is circling right there in front of me and the sun feels warm on my face. It's going to be all right. Help is on the way.

Suddenly the hawk gives a loud whistle, folds its wings, and dives out of sight. I shake myself. It's not over yet. I have to go back and tell Mr. Osgood that I've gotten through, and then help him get back down the trail.

But when I reach the trailhead, he's not there. He'd been hiding under this fallen cedar. He said he'd wait for me. This doesn't make any sense. All of the elation I'd been feeling is gone now, replaced with a sense of foreboding. This isn't good.

Calm down, Baron, I tell myself. Think. Do you have the wrong place?

I look around, trying to shake the confusion that has settled over me like a thick cloud. There are the two trail markers, right where I saw them before, nailed head high onto the pine tree a few yards away. But there is something different. I see something resting on the bare rock of the trail just past that pine. It's red. I walk over, and bend to pick it up with numb fingers. It's a kerchief stained with blood.

❧ 23 ❧

Stones

How does a human being turn into a bear-walker? One who can put on the skin of an animal? Maybe it's not the how that is as important as the why. Why would someone want to walk away from being human? I know there's no easy answer to this. There's probably more than one answer. To get something or to get away from something. Power and pain.

I'm not a trained tracker. Even though I'm Mohawk I've spent less time in the woods than the average Boy Scout. And just because I was born Indian doesn't mean I have the instinctual knowledge, like a spider that knows how to spin a web just because it's a spider. But I do have the things that my elders have been teaching me—two things in particular that I've been told by my parents, by great-uncle Jules, and by Grama Kateri. Look and Listen. Simple enough, it seems, but hard to do and do right.

I started looking and listening as soon as I found Mr. Osgood's bloody kerchief. I knew he hadn't dropped it by accident. It was weighed down by a stone so it would stay where it was out in plain sight. A marker. A decoy to draw away from my trail the one Mr. Osgood must have seen approaching up the mountain. When a person or an animal comes upon a flock of baby grouse, fluffy, vulnerable little things, the first thing that happens is that the mother grouse will hop out in plain sight. She'll be dragging one wing, which seems to be broken. And that person or hungry animal will concentrate on her because she seems such easy prey as she flops along, just barely keeping ahead of that predator. But it's all an act. When she's far enough away and the chicks have had time to escape, she'll leap up into flight.

Mr. Osgood, though, wasn't pretending to be hurt. I couldn't run away and leave him. That stone on his handkerchief had given me an idea. Off to the side of the trail was a scatter of other stones that had broken off a ledge. I searched through them, hefting them until I found several that fit my hand easily, all about the size of a lacrosse ball, but twice as heavy. I loaded my pockets, then I followed the trail that Mr.

Osgood had left. I didn't know what I could do to help, but I had to try.

And now that I've found the first place on a muddy section of the trail where a big footprint overlays Mr. Osgood's smaller boot print, I'm heartened just a little by what I see. Even though Walker White Bear's heart and spirit are twisted, his aims those of a pitiless predator, his footprints are still those of a human being.

I look around. I know this place well, a little too well. It's where the mother bear picked me up and tossed me aside like an unruly cub. I put a hand up to my aching shoulder. She hadn't meant to hurt me. If she'd wanted to do that, I wouldn't be standing here now. In a strange way, that pain in my shoulder felt reassuring, like a connection. If only it was. I could use the strength and size of a mother bear right now. Instead, all I have is the determination to do what I can to protect an old man I hardly know, but who already feels like an uncle to me.

I know that the mother bear and her two cubs should be miles from here by now. No way would they stick around with all the human activity. Although, on the other hand, bears are curious creatures and sometimes watch us humans as we stumble about in their forest, probably with amusement. I put my hand into my pocket and feel the little wooden bear. I don't bring it out. I just trace its outline with my thumb and forefinger.

"My relative," I say in a quiet voice, "take pity on me again. Help me if you can."

Do I see something dark and furry off to the side of my vision among the trees? I'm not sure, but I don't turn to look. I start down the trail. Somehow, despite his bad leg, Mr. Osgood has kept ahead so far. But I know it's just a matter of time before his bloodthirsty pursuer catches up to him. I have to hurry.

As it is, I almost hurry too much. Luckily, though, my ears save me.

"You can't escape me!"

At the sound of that voice so deep and growling it barely seems human, I stop myself just in time before I blunder around the turn in the steep trail just ahead. I drop low and look around the rock face. Just below me is a chilling scene. Mr. Osgood has fallen, his bad leg twisted under him. He's holding up a stick that he must have been using as a cane. It's not going to be much help against the wide-shouldered, hulking figure that is taking one slow step after another toward him.

"You're mine," the bearwalker growls again. His voice shakes the air around him like a rumble of thunder. He raises the saw-edged knife high in one hand, ready to slash down. It is as dramatic and terrifying as any scene from a horror film.

Until my first stone thwacking him in the back of his head spoils the effect. He doesn't fall, though. Goliath he might be, but I'm not doing as well in the part of David as I'd hoped. I've surprised him, but he's not even stunned. He whips his head around to stare up at me. His mouth gapes open to show those sharp teeth of his. His glare is so evil that it almost paralyzes me.

Not quite, though. I wing my second stone. He ducks to the side but it still glances off his cheek, drawing blood.

"Aaaargghhh," he roars.

But I refuse to be scared.

"Onyatgah!" I yell back in Mohawk. "Rancid meat!" It's an old insult that Grama Kateri taught me. I put all the scorn and contempt that I possibly can into my voice, knowing that will be even more insulting to one whose aim is to cause terror.

His leap in my direction is even faster than

I expect. Only the fact that I am uphill keeps him from reaching me, and the loose stones that he slips on are all that stop him from catching up to me. I turn and scramble back up the slope as fast as I can, the bearwalker close behind me, my death in his enraged eyes.

24

A Real Bear

Fast Runner. That is the name of one of the heroes in the old-time tales that Grama Kateri told me. His feet fly as he outdistances all those who would destroy him and catches up to those who would escape him.

Just staying ahead of the one who is after my blood is enough for me right now. I don't need to look back. I can hear him behind me. He's breathing hard, cursing like a human one moment and snarling like a wild creature the next. The fact that the trail is rough and twisting is helping me, but not as much as I'd hoped. As if I actually had that much of a plan when I started this. I'm not really climbing as fast as I can. I want him to stay close, not give up and then head back to finish off Mr. Osgood. But I don't want him to get close enough to grab me.

The trail is going to get wider soon, and level out more as it enters a small stretch of forest—hemlocks, birch trees, and a few maples. I hear him stumble behind me and fall back. I can't let him stop. I turn and look down at him. He's less than a stone's throw below. His shirt tore open against the rough edge of the cliff as he fell. Blood is trickling down his cheek from the place where my stone hit. I risk goading him on.

"Nyah-gwaheh?" I call back at the bearwalker. "Monster bear? Hunh. You're not a bear. You are a woodchuck."

He surges up from his knees after me. I wait for a heartbeat, then I turn and climb faster. Up and up. As I circle a broad shoulder of the mountain, I risk another glance back over my shoulders. I don't see him following, but I can hear the rattle of stones being dislodged by his heavy boots as he continues to climb. He's no more than fifty yards behind me.

I step up onto a shelf where enough earth has been cupped by the mountain for larger trees to grow. The way is wider now through this stretch of forest. I sprint forward—but only for a few steps before I stumble and barely right myself. Whatever energy I got from that power bar I ate and the adrenaline that has been surging through me has almost worn out. My knees are shaking as I rest my hands on them. The sun is already three hands high. I've been running all through the night and well into the morning. I'm not sure how much longer I can keep going. And I'm not sure how this race of mine is going to end. I have to stop.

I can't stop. I force my legs to move, stumble forward. But I don't get far. As I start past a huge hemlock something growls, leaps out, grabs at my leg, and knocks me into a roll that ends with me flat on my back.

A black-furred shape the size of a dog is rocking back and forth on its legs, its mouth open as if it is laughing at me. It's one of the two bear cubs. This is crazy. Wild bears just aren't supposed to behave this way. Does it really think I'm its brother now?

"Hunnrrrhhhh?" The little bear moans and rocks back and forth in front of me, raising up on its hind legs and waving its front paws at me. Come on. Let's play. It's so cute that I almost forget where I am for a second.

Thwomp! Yipe!

A big boot kicks the bear cub aside. It squeals in a high, loud voice as it lands and then lies there, curls up, and cries like a little baby. I don't think it's badly hurt. Bear cubs are tough.

I sit up and stare coldly at the one who did this. I'm not afraid now. I can feel a red rage growing and I know now that it is not just in my mind.

"I've got you now, you little squirt," his deep voice snarls.

The burly human whose mind is so twisted that he thinks himself as powerful as an evil creature out of an old story leers at me. He's holding his knife in one hand, his other hand reaching toward me. His eyes are narrowed as he takes a slow step. The grisly necklace of torn-out bear claws rattles against his chest.

"You have nothing," I say, "except for her. Time to meet a real bear."

I'm not sure he hears those last words of mine because the mother bear's angry charge hits him just then. He's hurled down and to the side. He's struck so hard by her four hundred pounds of muscle and bones, and infuriated teeth and claws, that his knife flies out of his hand. There's nothing more dangerous than a mother bear defending her cubs.

Jason Jones screams. His voice is no longer deep and threatening. He's not a figure of fear, a bearwalker. He's just a human being who has discovered at last how much less power he has than the natural world. Like most of those who seek to harm the weak, he's a coward at heart. His terrified voice is calling for help now over the growls of the mother bear, who is determined to make certain he will never kick one of her children again.

There is pity in my heart for him at this moment. I also know there's nothing I can do except this: stand up slowly, back away. By the time I reach the place where the trail dives down the rocky slope, the screaming has ended.

25

Rescuers

Mr. Osgood and I hear the pontoon chopper go overhead just before we reach the bottom of the trail. We've made pretty good time with him leaning both on his stick and my one good shoulder. The fact that he found a second power bar in his pocket for me to wolf down helped some, too. Defeating monsters does work up an appetite.

And before we even reach Camp Chuckamuck we are joined by three sheriff's deputies who have driven their pickup to the place where the road was blocked by the dynamite blast and then walked the rest of the way in. Whatever I said in my phone call must have been convincing. It has brought as much help as any of us might have wished.

More than we even needed.

"Stay back," one of the deputies is saying to us. A figure is starting toward us down the front steps of the main camp building.

"Shucks, young fella," Mr. Osgood says. "I'm not that afeared of my wife."

The deputy steps aside as Mrs. Osgood throws her arms around her husband and me both and squeezes hard. With our combined injuries it probably hurts him as much as it does me, but neither one of us complains.

"Thank you," Mrs. Osgood whispers to me.

After being greeted by Mrs. Osgood that way I'm only a little surprised at what I find when we follow the deputies into the building. Everyone is there and unharmed—aside from Mr. Mack, Cal, and Marlon, who appear to have suffered a considerable amount of bruising and are tied up in the corner. My midnight escape had provided the opportunity for Mr. Wilbur and Mrs. Osgood to put a couple of good-sized bumps on the heads of the distracted and dim brothers when Mr. Mack ran out after me. Mr. Wilbur had used a chair on Cal, but Mrs. Osgood had found a handier weapon. The fact that Poe-boy was engaged in taking a bite out of Marlon's leg had made it a bit easier for her to take aim.

"Dented my bear pan," Mrs. Osgood complains.

When Mr. Mack came back in, he found himself confronted by the sight of two incapacitated confederates, a large growling Labrador, and the pearl-handled pistol in the hands of Mr. Philo.

"I've got a shotgun," he'd said.

"Filled with rock salt, sonny" had been Mrs. Osgood's rejoinder from her hiding place behind the door, before she'd used her cast-iron bear pan to punctuate that remark.

"We looked for you for a good hour by the lake," Mr. Wilbur says, then explains how they decided—over his protests—to concentrate on keeping the other kids quiet and protected. After all, Jason Jones was still out there and the safest thing for everyone to do was to stay inside where the adults could keep all the doors and windows guarded.

"Once we heard that helicopter," Mr. Wilbur says, gesturing toward the rescue craft floating on its pontoons just beyond the dock where I fell into the water, "we knew you'd gotten through."

He pauses and looks at me. "Have you gotten taller?" he says. Then he laughs. "Baron, you have been through the mill! Talk about a rite of passage!" He reaches out a friendly hand and squeezes my shoulder. It's the same shoulder where the bear bit me. The colors around me are fading to gray. I start to sink toward the floor. I can hear voices shouting from far away. Then everything is dark and silent.

Coming Back

When I open my eyes, it's morning. At least I think it is. I feel like I'm coming back from someplace blurry and far away. My eyes don't want to open all the way. I feel groggy and confused. But I can tell that I'm not in Camp Chuckamuck. Everything around me is too white. No knotty pine paneling or rustic furnishings. Was everything that happened to me just a dream? Getting shot and bitten by a bear and chased by the bearwalker? Was all of that like one of those dreams I used to have when I was a little kid being chased by a monster until I woke up safe in my own bed?

Except this isn't my own bed. I try to push myself up and pain stabs through my shoulder where the mother bear's teeth sank into muscle and scraped bone. I think I hear someone saying something, but the words are indistinct.

"Don't . . . you're in . . ."

I fall back to the pillow and keep falling.

The next time I open my eyes, my eyelids don't stick like they have glue on them. I can see clearly and I'm sitting partway up in the hospital bed. Someone is holding my hand. When I see who it is, I know I'm dreaming.

"Mom?" I ask.

"You're awake," she says with a smile.

It's too good to be true. She leans over and hugs me and I don't even ask any of the questions that are filling my head right now because it's enough to just have her here.

Here, I soon discover, is Lake Placid Hospital. And here is where I have been for the last week, drifting in and out of consciousness. I'd been so beaten up and dehydrated and lost so much blood that the doctors were surprised I'd been able to walk, much less run, for miles along that mountain trail. Plus, in addition to the puncture wounds in my shoulder, which had been partially dislocated, I also got a roaring infection in the wounds on my back. Although I don't remember much at all, since I've been knocked out by the pain killers and the other stuff they had to pump into me.

The Army contacted my mother, and she's been given family leave and flown back home to be with me. She arrived two days ago and has been at my bed every since. She won't be going back to Iraq. She's been reassigned to a training job at Camp Drum here in upstate New York.

"You'll still be staying with Grama Kateri," she says. "It'll be a while before I can go back full-time to civilian life."

'That's okay," I say. "Grama Kateri is great."

"Plus you'll be able to stay at Pioneer Junior High where you've got all your friends," Mom adds.

"Huh?" I say. What friends? Does she mean Mr. Wilbur?

Mom reaches over and picks up a box. "You must be the most popular kid in your school," she says. "There's over thirty get-well letters here from your classmates. Plus there's that." She points with her chin toward the wall on the other side of my bed. There's a big sign pasted up there, eight feet long and four feet high, with two words on it in huge letters.

And all around it the kids in my class have signed their names and written stuff. Not just "Get well soon," but also things like "Baron, you rock!" and "I never knew you were so cool!"

I look back at Mom. For some reason my eyes are moist. She has her head turned sideways, studying me.

"Is it my imagination," she says, "or did you get bigger while I was gone?"

It's a bright December morning. It's warm for this time of year and there's no snow yet. The sun is shining on the steps of Grama Kateri's trailer, where I'm sitting and waiting for the school bus. I'm holding my little carved bear in one hand and my pen in the other as I write in my old journal. Mr. Wilbur gave it back to me yesterday. Between all that happened that last day at Camp Chuckamuck and my being in the hospital and then everything else, he completely forgot that he'd found it on the floor inside the main camp building. It fell out of my pocket when he gave me that friendly shoulder squeeze.

Reading through some of my old entries, it now seems to me as if I spent too much time feeling sorry for myself. But, like Grama Kateri says, remembering where you were helps you figure out where you need to go.

Where Mr. Mack and Cal and Marlon needed to go was to jail. They all accepted plea bargains that gave the brothers five to ten years in the crowbar hotel and Mr. Mack ten to fifteen. They could have taken their chances on a trial, but their lawyers advised them to take the deal that gave them shorter sentences. After all, Mr. Mack could have gotten a life sentence for attempted manslaughter. Their deal meant that they had to testify against the no-good nephews of the Philos and the executive officers of the Awlin Group, the developers who were behind the whole plot to destroy Camp Chuckamuck—and, though they are still trying to deny this part of it, eliminate Mr. and Mrs. Philo. Mr. Wilbur has told me that the case will be tied up in the courts for years, but it is probably going to end up bankrupting the Awlin Group, and that, sooner or later, almost all of the bad guys will end up in prison.

As for the Philos and Camp Chuckamuck,

there's good news there, too. Mr. and Mrs. Philo have decided that they're not ready to retire after all. They'll be hiring a new staff, but the Philos will be on site at the camp to make sure things get run right. They've also finished all the legal work to put the whole property into a permanent conservation easement to protect it from future development and keep it forever wild as a nature preserve. No logging. No condo or resort building. No matter what happens, its fifteen hundred acres will still be a place for the moose and the bears, the tall cedars and hemlocks, and all the other wildlife and plants of the Adirondack regions.

There's one or two more things you're probably wondering about. I know that I am.

The first, of course, is the monster at the heart of this story, the one who turned out to be a man with a painful past and a twisted heart. The Bearwalker. Walker White Bear or Jason Jones or whoever he was. What finally happened to him?

I'm sorry to say that's another question that hasn't been answered. The sheriff's deputies and the others who were called in to search looked for the place where Jones had been attacked by the mother bear. They only had Mr. Osgood's directions to go on since I was still in the hospital and in no condition to talk to anyone. And Mr. Osgood hadn't seen it for himself. He just passed on what I had told him as we limped down the mountain.

They never found the spot. No sign of a struggle, no trail of blood. No bear tracks. Nothing. Finally they called off the search. Only one thing ever turned up. In November a hiker on one of those high trails saw something half buried in the leaves. It was a rusty saw-bladed hunting knife. Maybe someday a big-boned skeleton with unusually long canine teeth in its skull will be found. Or maybe not.

Although my mom is back safe and sound, we still don't know what happened to my dad. It's been said that some American soldiers are being held as prisoners of war. All we can do is hope that he's one of them and that someday he will be able to come home. Uncle Jules says that life is like that. You never get an answer to every question. You just have to trust that you'll learn enough.

The bus driver is honking his horn at me. I look up. Tara is waving from one window of the bus and Cody is gesturing at me from the window behind hers. It's a toss-up which one of them I'll sit with today. Maybe Tara. After all, I'll see plenty of Cody at basketball practice after school. Even though I'm the shortest guy on the team, I'm the fastest down the court and I have a great jump shot. Plus I'm now five foot six and I'm still growing.

Enough. Time to close this journal and end this story. At least for now.

JOSEPH BRUCHAC is the author of SKELETON MAN, THE RETURN OF SKELETON MAN, THE DARK POND, WHISPER IN THE DARK, and BEARWALKER, as well as many other critically acclaimed novels, poems, and stories, many drawing on his Abenaki heritage. Mr. Bruchac and his wife, Carol, live in upstate New York, in the same house where he was raised by his grand-parents. Visit him online at www.josephbruchac.com.